Alicia's Possession

Colette L. Saucier

First Print Edition: August 2013
ISBN-13: 978-0615875521
ISBN-10: 0615875521

E-book ISBN: 978-0-9967272-0-4

Cover design by Dawné Dominique
Edited by Julie Reilly

Dedication

To Valerina, Patia, and Sondra – *Cheers, ladies!*

Chapter One

The house on Lilac Lane did not speak to Mason as he rounded the cul de sac and spied the front porch through the sparse woods, not far from the road. His tires crunched upon gravel as he turned his car along the circular drive. He had always prided himself on his uncanny knack of being able to assess the inhabitants whenever he was called out, but not tonight. The nondescript façade remained tightlipped, perhaps smirking at him—sent on a fool's errand. He hadn't been out on a suspicious incident call since he'd been out of uniform, but power had its privileges. If a congressman's daughter got spooked by a firecracker, send a detective out to do a deputy's job.

Mason pulled up alongside the Audi parked outside the closed garage, and the outside light brightened as it detected his motion walking up the front steps. He pressed the doorbell but became impatient after half a minute with no response. As he rapped his knuckles on the ten-foot heavy oak door, he almost wished he were still in uniform so he'd have a nightstick for knocking. The door opened to reveal a lanky man, perhaps six feet four, with deep-set eyes and thinning salt and pepper hair.

"Mr. Pageant?" Mason asked him.

"No, Pageant is my wife's maiden name. I'm John Meador. Dr. Meador." He opened the door further for Mason to enter.

"Detective Crawley. I understand you think you heard gunshots?"

"Not exactly. I'm afraid you might have been called out unnecessarily. Can I get you some coffee? I assume you can't drink on the job."

"Thanks, no. What do you mean, 'not exactly'?"

"My wife thinks she heard gunshots, from across the lake."

Meador walked through to a bar set up against one of the few walls in the open floor plan, and Mason followed. The house had been tastefully decorated with furniture expensive enough to appear inviting and comfortable. A plush mocha suede couch divided the living space, and artwork and artifacts from around the globe graced the walls, shelves, and tables. Long windows interspersed with French doors ran along two walls. Although the twilight inhibited the view of the water, Mason knew the narrow bend of the lake bordered the house on both sides, and he stared out beyond the glass toward the dimly-lit homes on the other side.

"So you didn't hear anything?"

"No, I wasn't here at the time, but I'm sure it was nothing."

"What makes you think that?" Mason asked, facing the man who stood jingling the ice in his rocks glass.

"Do you know about my wife's accident?" When Mason shook his head, Meador continued. "It was in the news. Car accident. She was in a coma for nearly two months. She's only been home from the hospital a few weeks, but with the head injury combined with the drugs she takes for the headaches—plus, I think she was drinking with her medication—I don't think we can place too much trust in anything she might say."

Just keeps getting better and better. Maybe he should take him up on the offer of a drink since there was no job here to do. "Can I speak with your wife?"

"She's changing. She'll be out in a minute."

"When did the alleged incident occur?"

"I think around two, she said."

"This afternoon?"

"No, this morning. She says it woke her up."

"Why didn't you report it earlier?"

"I wanted to," said a female voice behind them, "but John spent all day trying to talk me out of it."

Mason turned to face the woman and knew one thing immediately—she did not belong with that man. At least a full decade younger. Petite with dark hair, chocolate eyes with irises almost as dark as the pupils dilated in their center, pink lips perfect for kissing, and pale skin, which warmed with a blush that quickly receded. Pretty—almost too pretty, and could have been cut from that superficial socialite/debutante cloth if it weren't for the profound sadness emanating from her, giving her depth. A woman-child with the appearance of vulnerability, of needing protection. More than likely, someone would need protecting from her.

She stood before Mason without him even registering that she had walked toward him, although he hadn't taken his eyes off her, and extended her hand. "I'm Alicia Pageant."

"Detective Crawley," he said. Her grip was firmer than he would have expected from such small, soft hands, and he noted her use of her father's name, already wielding her birthright of authority. Still, he released her hand reluctantly. "Congressman Pageant's daughter?"

"The former—not the current. After my father's death, his wife assumed the position, but my step-mother and I are not on the best of terms. But I won't bore you with stories of family dysfunction."

"Er, yes." Although not one to keep up with politics—or even much news—Mason had a vague recollection of Congressman Pageant going down in his Cessna several years back and his young wife being appointed to his seat, but she was correct. That had nothing to do with why he was there. "You reported hearing gunshots."

"John thinks I imagined it, but I know what I heard—and what I saw."

"You saw something? I thought the sound of shots woke you up."

"John, would you get me a glass of Bordeaux please?"

John met Mason's eyes with a tilt of his head and brows raised. "Should you be drinking with your medication?"

"Damn it, John, I can handle a glass of wine." She turned and flopped on the couch with an impatient sigh. Resting her elbow on the arm of the couch, she closed her eyes and laid her head against her palm.

Mason took the chair to her left and leaned toward her. "Maybe you should listen to him. He is a doctor."

She laughed and glanced up at him with unsmiling eyes. "I haven't turned to stone. Yet. He's a doctor of geology." Under her breath, she added, "Pretentious prick."

Meador handed her a glass filled halfway with dark crimson wine. "Here you are, darling."

She rolled her eyes. "Thanks," she said and took a sip then turned her attention back to Mason. "The shots woke me up, but this morning I watched them."

"Who?"

"The neighbors. The woman who lives across the lake, or her accomplice I suppose."

Her husband scoffed and shook his head. "Where were you, Dr. Meador?" Mason asked.

"He doesn't live here," Alicia answered for him. "We're getting a divorce."

"We're just taking some time apart," John said, but Alicia shook her head.

"Mrs. Mea…Pageant," Mason said, "please just tell me what happened."

Alicia stared past the detective toward the French doors as she recalled the events of the previous night. Then she glanced down at the wine glass cupped in her palms, a twin of the one she had been holding that evening.

She had poured a glass of Bordeaux, grabbed her Kindle, and made her way out to the sofa on the terrace. An imminent headache would preclude her reading soon enough, but for the time being, she wanted to enjoy the solitude and the surroundings, as much as it was possible for her to find pleasure in anything. Fingers of light through the trees from the setting sun cast glitter across the lake, and a chorus of frogs, crickets, and cicadas provided the background music.

Perhaps half an hour had passed when the yelling disrupted her peace, not the first time she had heard the couple who occupied the house at a slight diagonal across from hers screaming at each other. Although she could not make out the words, being privy to such intimacies made her uncomfortable and, for some reason, embarrassed—an unwitting interloper to their strained relationship.

Alicia attempted to focus on her novel, but both the pitch and the volume of the woman's voice continued to rise just before the crash of breaking glass rang out. She flinched at the sound then imagined what it might have been. A vase? Liquor bottle? Wedding china? The plot of her novel couldn't compete with the drama across the lake. Unable to tolerate her own eavesdropping any longer, she retreated into the house.

She didn't know what time she had fallen asleep while reading in bed, but when she was awoken by an echoing crack, her eyes popped open wide and went straight to the clock. 2:13. Before she could close them again, a second shot rang out. Was it a gunshot?

She sat up in bed, her hand reflexively rising to cover the throbbing pain on the side of her head. The third shot erupted, she thought from across the lake, but how could she be certain?

She stood up and peeked around the curtains of her bedroom window, the house of the arguing couple clearly visible with most of its interior lights on. Odd for this time of night, but perhaps the shots had awoken them as well. Then, one by one, each light went out, and the house disappeared into the darkness.

Her head still pounding, she walked into the kitchen area and turned on the light to get her Ultram and a glass of water then became keenly aware that anyone outside could see her, fully illuminated, through the surrounding windows. She flipped off the switch and grabbed her cell phone, debating whether or not to call 911. What could she tell them, really? She couldn't even be certain it had been gunfire or where it had originated. She recalled the photographs from the Kennedy assassination with heads turned and fingers pointing toward the grassy knoll—a misdirection that fueled conspiracy theories even to this day. Heavy with pain and exhaustion, she decided she lacked the motivation to get dressed and deal with policemen for uncertainties. She double-checked the burglar alarm then went back to bed with phone in hand.

Alicia tried to remain still, willing her headache to go away, for the pain pill to take effect, but she could only doze off and on. Not long after she'd gotten back into bed, another noise pulled her from it, and she stood once again, still groggy and rubbing her eyes, staring out her bedroom window across the lake. A silhouette emerged from the side of the house, struggling to carry what appeared to be a large duffel bag. The car parked beside the house had its trunk open, and the shadow hefted its load into it and slammed it shut. Alicia watched as the shadow disappeared into the house before she returned to bed.

When the dawn began to creep through her curtains, her desire for coffee surpassed her dedication to sleep. Since being released from the hospital, Alicia had come to enjoy drinking her coffee outside by the lake with the newspaper, but before she made her way out to the terrace, her attention was once again drawn to the neighbors as someone walked out of the house, climbed into the car, and drove away. Alicia returned to her morning routine and was sitting outside with the thick Sunday paper when the car rolled up a few hours later, and the woman she recognized as one of the occupants got out and went inside. Alone. Over the course of the morning, Alicia kept an eye out for the husband—she assumed it was her husband—and though she could see the woman's form milling about in and around the house, he never returned.

Mason had listened to her story, jotting down a handful of notes and only interrupting a few times to ask for clarification on a particular point.

"I had decided to call the sheriff's office," she said, "but then John got here and said I shouldn't bother, that it's probably nothing."

"He's probably right," Mason said. The combination of pain killers and wine, being alone, too many movies or police procedurals, had more than likely fed her imagination. "So you've never met the couple before?"

"Um…no, they must have moved in while…"

"They moved in while Alicia was still in a coma," Meador said in a condescending tone.

Alicia's gaze dropped to the glass in her hand, her cheeks flushed. "Yes, John, I was in a coma. I had a head injury. But that does not change what I saw or the fact that I have heard them arguing repeatedly or that I heard gunshots."

"What you think were gunshots."

Mason closed his notepad and stood up. "Mr. Meador, you're probably right, but it won't hurt for me to go over and ask a few questions.

Alicia jumped to her feet and came close to colliding with Mason—close enough for him to catch her clean scent with a hint of honeysuckle—and he stopped just short of grabbing her arm. "But don't you need to investigate or something?" she asked. "Won't she be suspicious?"

"If I understand what you're saying, you think that the wife shot her husband then got someone to help her move the body."

"You don't believe me."

"I believe that's what you think happened, but more than likely there's a more reasonable explanation. I'll just go and tell her that there was a report of gunfire in the area and ask if she heard anything." When his eyes met hers, he could see the disappointment reflected in them before her thick black lashes fluttered down as she dropped her gaze to the floor. "I have your contact number. I'll let you know what she says."

She nodded and stepped away from him, taking another sip of her wine. "Thank you for your time, Detective. I hope I'm not sending you on some wild goose chase."

"Well, I hope you are." When she turned and frowned at him, he said, "Think of the alternative, that a man has been killed."

Her face relaxed and the corners of her mouth raised a fraction of an inch. "I suppose you're right. Let's hope I'm wrong."

Meador walked Mason to the door, but before he walked out, he turned back for one last, lingering look. "Goodnight, Ms. Pageant. I'll be in touch."

"Why don't you go, too, John," Alicia said.

He blinked back and scowled. "I thought you might want me to stay over tonight."

"Oh?"

"I didn't think you'd want to be alone after this gunshot incident."

She set her glass down on the kitchen island and tilted her head. "Really? But I thought you were so certain I imagined the whole thing!"

"Um, uh…" He looked at his shoes.

"Please just go. Which reminds me, why did you come over here to begin with?"

"I, uh, needed a book from my study."

"Next time, call first. And bring some boxes. It's

time you got the rest of your stuff out of here."

"Alicia, be reasonable."

She shook her aching head. "No, don't you dare tell me to be reasonable. I'm not the one who cheated." He reached for her hand, but she crossed her arms. "Just go."

He exhaled an exaggerated sigh and stormed out of the house, slamming the door and not taking any book. Its echo still hung in the air when the intonations of Skype joined it, and Alicia walked over to the nook that housed her laptop and printer. She sat down and rubbed her hands over her face and over her head before clicking the mouse to take her sister's call.

"Hi, Maddie," she said in as cheery a tone as she could muster, which sounded disingenuous to her own ears. "How is Colombia?"

"Hot, as usual." Maddie's voice rang through clear, although her image on screen jumped around distractedly. "How are you?"

"I...I'm all right, I guess. Still having headaches, but that's to be expected."

"How are you dealing with the situation between you and John?"

That familiar tightness gripped Alicia's chest and throat, and she knew if she allowed herself to think about it for too long, she wouldn't be able to hold back the tears. "It hasn't been easy. How did I handle it the first time around?"

"Sorry, Leash. Wish I could tell you. He's just a fucking asshole. You do realize that. Don't you? This is about him—not you. You've just got to believe that."

Alicia dropped her head onto her palm and wished she weren't on a webcam. "I wish I could. I thought we were happy."

"It's his problem—not yours."

"There must be something wrong with me, something lacking. I wasn't enough. Why wasn't I enough for him?" She couldn't hold back the slow tears that slid silently down her cheek. "I wish I'd never come out of that coma." She didn't say what she knew Maddie could infer. She wished she'd never been pulled out of that lake at all. Although Alicia had no memory of the accident, she thought of it as a metaphor for her life—careening out of control and thrusting her into an unfamiliar domain of cold, pain, and darkness.

"Alicia, don't say that. Come on. You can get through this. You're a beautiful, vital, intelligent, incredible woman. Don't let this one dickhead ruin your life."

She lifted her head, sniffed, and returned her focus to her sister's fragmented image. "Do you know how many years I wasted with that man? Years of my life when maybe I could have been pursuing my own dreams, or finding someone who would think I'm enough for him!"

"You have got to stop thinking like this."

Alicia lifted her eyes to the ceiling and shook her head. "It's not that simple."

"I just want you to be happy."

"Don't you think I would be if I could? I can't just snap my fingers and stop being depressed, and your pressuring me is not helping. Listen, I'm hungry. I need to go order something to eat."

"You're still not leaving the house? That's not healthy, Alicia."

"Goodnight, Maddie." She clicked the mouse without waiting for her sister to say goodbye.

Alicia poured another glass of wine and pulled a Chinese delivery menu out of a kitchen drawer. She opened one of the French doors leading out to the terrace but stopped when she heard indistinct voices coming from the other side of the lake. Although she couldn't make out what he was saying, she recognized the timbre of the detective's voice as he spoke to the woman. Then, illuminated by the outside lights, he gestured in her direction and the woman looked her way. Alicia jumped back, out of their sight.

She gulped from her wine without tasting then noted her hand around the glass, recalling how it had warmed within the detective's firm grip. Still steering clear from view, she dropped the menu and plucked his card from the kitchen island. Mason Crawley. She had liked his look, in a way she hadn't since…since before she could remember. Had she imagined the flicker of attraction that sparked between them? Almost a palpable vibration, like being paged at a restaurant when her table was ready. She tapped the card against her teeth. She thought it smelled of him—woods and spice—but then realized his scent had lingered on her hand. She thought of those strong hands upon her bare back, and a fevered shiver ran through her, catching her breath.

What difference did it make, really? He had pierced her with his dark blue eyes, as deep and turbulent as the ocean, but she noticed, too, the doubt, the incredulity. Whether he believed her or not, she'd likely never see him again—and be better off for it. A woman could lose herself in those eyes. The last thing she wanted was another man in her life—or anyone, for that matter. To open herself up to the risk of betrayal. To allow herself to be vulnerable again. No, the hurt was too deep, the pang too severe. In addition to her chronic headaches, she had the constant sensation of a knife stuck into her back just below her left shoulder blade. All she had known, everything she had believed about her marriage, her life— her...self!—all lies. She stood powerless on the sidelines as it all spun out of her control.

She could never forgive the man she had married even if it had been only a few times—or even once. Even if it had been over months ago, as he said. Too many ifs—too many doubts. Facing it when she came home from the hospital was like learning of his infidelity for the first time—she'd been stung by the same hornet twice. No, she couldn't imagine exposing herself to that kind of pain again, at least for a while. Perhaps forever. The wounds had not yet scarred, as if the accident had torn off the scab, ripped out the stitches, leaving her raw and bleeding. She didn't see how she could ever trust a man again, no matter how blue his eyes.

She glanced out past the windows, peering into the darkness, but she couldn't make out anyone at the house across the lake, and the cars were no longer parked in the drive. She walked back toward the door and started to close it, but at the moment she touched the knob, her phone rang, making her jump.

Although she didn't recognize the number, she

answered anyway. "He-hello?"

"Ms. Pageant? This is Detective Crawley."

She cleared her throat to dislodge the lump that had formed when she heard his voice. "Y-yes?" A wave of heat flooded her face, embarrassed as if he somehow knew she'd been thinking about him.

"Just wanted to let you know that I spoke with your neighbor—Judith Holloman. Says her husband—Danny, or Daniel—left early this morning on an overseas business trip. She was kind of vague on the details, so I'm going to check it out, but more than likely that's what you saw."

She closed her eyes and rubbed the temple where a headache had begun to take root. "But what about the gun shots?"

"Says her husband was shooting a snake."

"A snake?"

"Yeah, evidently he's ex-Marine. A sharpshooter. Said he was outside by the lake, saw a snake, and killed it. From what I gather, he does this frequently, or whenever they spot a snake."

"Did you see it?"

"See what?"

"The snake. Did he kill it? Did you see its body?"

He said nothing for several moments. "Ms. Pageant, I investigate homicides of people—not snakes."

I bet some of the people you investigate are snakes, she thought. "But if you didn't see the dead snake, how do you know that's what happened?"

The impatience in his sigh carried through the phone. "Listen, I said I'm going to check out her story and confirm that her husband really is on a business trip. That should tell us if there is anything to investigate."

Despite understanding the logic, she couldn't suppress the gnawing discontent, but she'd have to be satisfied with that explanation for now.

"She did say something odd, though," he said, "and I had hoped you might be able to clarify something. You said you've never met your neighbors, they moved in while you were in the hospital."

"That's right."

"Mrs. Holloman said they've been living there for six months. She said you and she have met on many occasions."

The blood drained from her upper body, leaving her cold and her face tingling. Before she could formulate an explanation, or he could even ask for one, the doorbell rang. "I—I'm sorry, Detective, someone's at the door. I'll have to speak with you later." She ended the call without giving him a chance to respond.

Alicia stood frozen in the kitchen, staring at the phone in her hand for a full minute until the doorbell rang again and pulled her out of her stupor. As she walked to the door, she had no notion of who might be on the other side, but she had to fight back her shocked reflex to slam it shut when she found her neighbor on the porch holding a bottle of Malbec.

"Alicia." The woman's smile lit up her eyes. "I guess you don't remember me. I'm Jude." She held up the bottle. "Wine?"

Mason had no reason to return to Lilac Lane that night, and certainly none to sit in his parked car watching the house with its stoic veneer. He thought at first his attraction to Alicia had pulled him there like steel to a magnet. When he called, he tried to imagine where she was in the house as they spoke. The Audi was gone, the husband along with it, so she must be alone. He pictured her standing in front of the suede sofa where she'd been when they'd almost collided.

Although his meeting with the neighbor had created more questions than it answered, he'd had no doubt he would get to the bottom of it—that is, until he saw the Holloman woman's car pull up the drive. He kept his eyes on her as she walked toward the house, and he waited with his cell pressed against his ear for Alicia to tell him why she'd said she didn't know her.

"I—I'm sorry, Detective," she said, her voice soft and shaky. "Someone's at the door. I'll have to speak with you later." And the line went dead.

As he watched Mrs. Holloman disappear into the house, he knew his instincts had driven him to the house and not his libido. "What are they up to?"

Chapter Two

Mason hated math, especially when things didn't add up. That'd teach him to pinch hit on a Sunday shift. This *suspicious incident* should have been resolved in two phone calls. After faxing a request for Holloman's military records Monday morning, he'd even waited four days before following up, if only to prove to himself he had no unreasonable interest in the case, forcing the image of Alicia's face from his mind each time it invaded his thoughts.

Yes, the man had been a highly-decorated sharpshooter in the Marines, but so far, Mason couldn't find anyone to confirm that Daniel Holloman had crossed the street, let alone left the country. Mason's contacts at the airport and Homeland Security found no record of someone by that name on any departing flight on Sunday. Judith Holloman had been ambiguous at best as to her husband's destination—"Somewhere in Asia"—and said she had no way to reach him and no idea when he would return. She had stated her husband worked for Criterion Services and given Mason a business card, but when he called the number, he was told employee records were confidential. Only after he pressed the point of it being a police matter did the man on the other end of the call agree to have Holloman's supervisor call him back—*if* Holloman was in fact even an employee.

Slamming down the receiver in frustration, Mason turned to the computer on his desk and typed in the company web address. After half a minute:

> *The connection has timed out*
> *The server at www.criterionservices.com is taking too long to respond.*

What. The. Fuck?

"Hey, Buzz," he called out to the detective sitting at the desk diagonal from his.

"Yep?"

"Ever heard of Criterion Services?"

"Nope."

A Google search proved futile—only the same website with the same infuriating results.

Sunday night, Mason had watched the house on Lilac Lane far longer than was rational, especially considering he had no reason to watch it at all. Judith Holloman had remained only half an hour, but twenty minutes after she drove away, a gray Ford Focus rolled up the gravel drive. A man had climbed out of the car with a large brown paper bag, walked up and rung the bell, then handed the bag to Alicia Pageant before taking off.

Mason pulled out his notes with the license number and plugged them into the database. The car was registered to a middle-aged Chinese woman by the name of Mei Chéng. What would Alicia be receiving from Asians, and why did she deny knowing Judith Holloman when clearly she did?

"Hey, Mason, did you interview that witness in the Irwin case?" Buzz asked.

"Yeah, check the case notes. Do you know anything about Congressman Pageant's daughter being in a car crash a few months back?"

"Do I look like a traffic cop to you?"

Mason returned to the search engine and typed in *Alicia Pageant Meador*. A slew of society and faculty articles popped up, as well as an ancient catalog of the misadventures of her youth played out before the media—the Congressman's wild child. Nuisance charges—drunk and disorderly, underage drinking, possession of a joint. Destruction of property— keying an ex-boyfriend's car at the age of sixteen. The tales for tabloid fodder dried up once she went to the New York School of Interior Design, as if living at home had provided less structure than being cut loose on the streets of Manhattan.

Then he found the three-month-old news story about the accident.

Congressman's Daughter Hospitalized after Crashing into Campus Lake

A photo of a mangled BMW partially submerged in the water accompanied the headline. From the condition of the vehicle, Mason knew Alicia was lucky to be alive and unscarred. Not a mark on that perfect porcelain skin. Mason skimmed the article—single-car, only passenger, serious condition. The police spokesman was quoted as saying, "Alcohol is possibly a factor."

Mason minimized the browser and opened the official reporting system to pull up the crash report. He scanned the screen, translating the codes in his head.

Not Ejected. Trapped: Extricated. Airbag: Not Deployed. Shoulder and Lap Belt Used. Injury: Incapacitating/Severe. Condition of Driver: Had Been Drinking/Impaired.

But under "Alcohol/Drug Involvement," the officer had noted that no alcohol was present and no blood alcohol test had been given. The only violation listed was "careless operation."

Before Mason could try to track down the investigating officer, his phone rang. He answered it with, "Crawley."

"This is Jack Wright, contract specialist with DCMA," came the quick clipped speech on the other end of the line. "Understand you were asking about Daniel Holloman."

"Yes, we received a report of suspicious activity at his house, and I needed to conf—"

"Mr. Crawley, this is a security matter for DCMA."

"It's *Detective* Crawley. You're with DCMA?" Mason typed the initials into the search engine.

"I must advise you to stop your investigation into

the whereabouts of Holloman immediately."

"Can you confirm—" But a dial tone already rang in his ear.

Top results of his search: *DCMA | Defense Contract Management Agency*

He clicked the link.

> *The Defense Contract Management Agency (DCMA) is the Department of Defense (DOD) component that works directly with Defense suppliers...*

What had he stumbled into?

Mason pushed the doorbell then banged on the oak door without waiting. Alicia opened the door and stood in the threshold in a long silk Asian-patterned robe. Her damp hair hung in ringlets around her face and emitted that faint, familiar fragrance of honeysuckle. Damn, she was pretty, and although the blush that tinged her cheeks implied guilt, she was no femme fatale.

"Detective Crawley," she said as she stepped back to allow his entrance. "I wasn't expecting you." She closed the door then pulled her robe tighter around her. "You caught me just out of the shower. Mind if I change?"

"This shouldn't take long, Miss Pageant." He forced his gaze to the high ceilings, around the windows, across the living area, anywhere except her—where it most wanted to rest.

"Please, call me Alicia. Miss Pageant sounds like…someone else. Someone I used to be."

Mason faced her then. Lovely, luscious Alicia, with lips he could lick for days. Her hands trembled within the oversized sleeves. Was it nerves or a chill from just coming from the shower with nothing but that thin layer of silk over her skin. The robe did little to conceal her hardened nipples, and he tore his focus away while he still could.

"Did you find something out?" she asked.

"The only thing that's been consistent is that you haven't been completely forthcoming." His eyes followed as she swept across the room to the kitchen island and lifted a wine glass to her mouth with a shaky grasp.

"I don't know what you mean. I told you everything I heard, what I saw. Did you find Mr. Holloman? Is he all right?"

He focused on her face, her lips, her eyes. "Why don't you tell me?"

"What are you talking about?"

Mason stepped into her space the way he usually did to coerce a confession from a suspect, but her scent could have brought him to his knees. "You say you don't know the Hollomans, but Judith Holloman says she's known you for months."

"I…I don't recall ever having met her." Her words trailed out on an exhalation as her shallow breathing quickened.

"Why did she come here that night?"

"What?"

"She was here—Sunday night. Why?"

"I don't know. Just to visit."

"To visit! You thought she'd killed her husband!"

"But you said she hadn't!" Her eyes glazed over with unshed tears magnifying her chocolate eyes, making them even larger and darker than he had thought possible.

Usually this was where he wanted them; usually this was where they'd fold, but he caught himself not wanting to break her—not yet. And not like this. Instead, he had to restrain the instinct to comfort her.

Mason straightened his spine in an attempt to tower over her and peppered her with questions. "What are you not telling me? Why is the Department of Defense involved? Who was the man who came over after she left?"

She scowled and shook her head, freeing a tear to run down her cheek. "I know nothing about the Department of Defense, and I don't know who you're talking about. Were you watching my house?"

"He brought you something in a brown paper bag."

After a moment's thought, she sniffed and rolled her eyes. "You call yourself a detective." She spun around, jerked a drawer open, yanked out a sheet of paper, and shoved it into his chest.

Mason stared down at the folded pamphlet. *Kung Pao Kitchen*. Take out. Well, now he felt like an ass. When he looked up, he expected to find her expression full of derision, but instead she had tears streaming down her face.

He tossed the menu aside. "Why bring *me* into this?"

"I don't know what you mean."

"You used your influence, your daddy's name to

have a detective come out instead of a patrol car. Didn't you?"

"Yes—I don't like cops. They've never been nice to me."

He thought of all those tabloid headlines—the parties and petty arrests, how the beat cops might have resented a poor little rich girl.

"What do you want?" she asked. "I don't know what you want from me."

Mason gripped her upper arms, forcing her eyes to meet his. He knew he'd made a mistake the moment her warmth bled through the silk of her robe and into his palms, sending a ripple of sensation up his arms and down his body. "Why did you lie about knowing Judith?" he asked, his voice low and gravelly but not in the terse tone he used to intimidate a witness. No, she might not recognize it, but he could hear his lust cradling each syllable.

She squeezed her eyes tight as if to prevent her tears' escape, but instead it forced them down her cheeks. "I wasn't lying. I don't know her. I don't remember her. I don't remember anything."

He lifted one hand from her arm and brushed the tears from her cheek with his thumb before running it across her bottom lip. Her eyes remained closed, and his chest rose and fell in rhythm with hers. He leaned in close enough to inhale her breath.

"Don't," she said without force.

He shuffled his feet forward the few inches required for his body to brush against her breasts. "How can you not remember?"

"Th-the accident."

He brought his mouth down, barely touching hers,

his tongue tasting the salt of tears on her lips—those lips he had wanted to kiss from the first moment they'd met.

"Please," she said on a puff of air and tried to pull away from him, but he tightened his hold on her arm.

"Please what?"

"Please…don't kiss me."

"I think you want me to kiss you." When she said nothing in protest, he pressed his lips to hers and gently pulled first her top, then her bottom lip into his mouth. He held her chin between his thumb and fist to lift her face.

Tears still streamed down her cheeks, but she opened her eyes and shook her head. "I…I can't do this."

Mason trailed his finger down her throat to the opening of her robe, stopping just over her heart, and she trembled with a hitch in her breath.

"What do you mean you didn't remember her because of the accident?"

"I have…gaps, memory loss." Her tears had begun to wane.

"I'm going to kiss you again."

"No," she whispered when his mouth hovered mere millimeters over hers. He dropped his hand from her arm to the small of her back and pulled her against him, and she gasped at the unmistakable evidence of his arousal. "I'm not ready for this."

"Because of your injury?"

"Because of the infidelity. My husband. He hurt me." Her words pinched his heart and he nodded. "I can't *be* with a man—any man. I can't trust anyone. I don't even trust myself to have the sense or judgment to know who can be trusted. I don't know if I'll ever be able to trust anyone again."

Mason laid a soft kiss on her mouth, tugging her bottom lip gently between his teeth. He lifted his face just enough to look at her. In time, he could teach her to trust again, at least to trust him, but it would take patience—and perseverance. He thought she might be worth the effort.

"If you want me to stop," he told her, "if you really mean it, say 'apple.'"

Alicia furrowed her brow and blinked before meeting his stare directly. "But I told you to stop."

"Yes, but you didn't mean it." The color rushing into her cheeks proved him right. "I will only stop if you say 'apple.' Understand?"

She responded with a single, slow nod, never taking her eyes off him. When he covered her mouth with his, he ran his tongue along the seam of her lips, and she opened for him. He wrapped both arms around her then, holding her tight, and she placed her hands on his shoulders. As his tongue swirled inside her mouth, she leaned against him and released a low, moaning sigh. He allowed the kiss to continue and to deepen, in part because he wanted to prevent her from using the safety word, but primarily because he didn't want to relinquish her delicious mouth. Although he would never call himself a connoisseur, he could detect the subtle notes of cherry, chocolate, and plum from the wine on her tongue.

Mason walked her backward a few steps to bring her against the wall, and he leaned against her, his hardness pressing between her legs. He reached for the ends of the silk belt and pulled, allowing the robe to drape loose around her, and he slipped his hands in and rested them around her waist. He rubbed against her with only the fabric of his slacks between them, quickening the rise and fall of her breasts, her hardened nipples brushing his chest.

His hand began a slow descent to the core of her heat, but she pulled her mouth from his, as if breaking a magnetic force, and in a raspy voice said, "Apple."

Mason pulled her robe closed as he took a step back, and he tied the belt in a loose bow. They stood panting and staring at each other, and Mason traced a finger from her temple to her swollen lips. "You can trust me," he said. "The question is, can I trust you?"

What the hell was she doing? Alicia rushed into her bedroom and pulled on her jeans, not even bothering with underwear—willing to go commando in the interest of speed—then tossed around lingerie in an effort to find a bra. Just earlier that day, she had convinced herself she wanted nothing to do with men and couldn't imagine even wanting to kiss anyone, and here she had been ready to have sex with this detective right there on the kitchen floor! She knew nothing about him. He could be married, for all she knew. How ironic if she were to become the "other woman." And where the hell was a bra? She groaned in frustration and slammed the drawer shut.

"What's wrong?" Mason asked, leaning against the doorframe with his eyes following her.

"It's—it's nothing." She stepped into the closet and, dropping her robe, pulled a sweater over her head. That should suit her modesty. *Damn it*. A headache had launched its nightly invasion. She turned around and nearly ran into Mason. "What are you doing in my bedroom?"

"We still need to talk."

"I think you need to go."

"We're not having sex tonight, if that's what concerns you."

Heat bloomed in her cheeks, and she pushed past him. "I don't even know you, *Detective*. I have no desire to have sex with you."

"We both know that's not true. And you may call me Mason. For now."

She covered her burning face with her hands. "Please go."

"Come here," he said, but she didn't move. He took a step toward her, extending his hand. "I said, come here. Take my hand."

Alicia didn't know why she obeyed, but she dropped her hands from her cheeks, walked over to him, and placed her fingers upon his palm. He squeezed them gently and smiled. "Happy?" she asked with an arched brow.

"Very much so." He kissed her fingers then tugged her closer to him. "You're a natural."

"A natural what?"

"In time. Now go get your shoes on. I'm taking you to dinner. You have virtually no food in this house."

"I…I can't." What was it about this man that made her constantly stumble over speech? "Lately I keep misplacing things. I can't find any of my bras."

"Perhaps I'm not such a crap detective after all."

"What do you mean?"

"I already found your bras. Is there a reason you have them in your refrigerator?"

Pulling her hand free from his, she shook her head as she stomped out and into the kitchen, dragging her fingers through her damp curls before yanking open the refrigerator. There they were, lined up like a chilly, pastel jury rendering their verdict. She swallowed hard and inhaled back the tears that threatened to reemerge then closed the door and leaned her forehead against it. The heat off Mason preceded him, so Alicia didn't start when he placed his hand on her shoulder. "Please go."

"I told you, I'm taking you to dinner. I think those bras have chilled enough. Don't you?"

"Please don't make me. Do I have to say 'apple' not to go to dinner?"

"No, but you *do* have to tell me what's going on."

"You're going to think I'm out of my mind."

Mason pulled her away from the refrigerator and turned her to face him. "I'll make you a deal. We won't go out if you promise to answer my questions—honestly. Now get those things out of the fridge, and I'll see if you have enough food to scrounge up a meal. How do you survive like this?"

"I have a woman who comes in once a week," she said as she raked her lingerie out of the refrigerator. "She brings me any staples I need, and I order take out a lot."

When Alicia returned from depositing her bras in her room, she found that Mason had closed all the blinds of the windows facing out onto the lake and was now scrounging through the pantry and cabinets.

"Are you off duty, or do you always kiss and cook for your witnesses?" she asked.

"That's the serve part of 'To serve and protect,'" he said, turning to her with a smile.

"May I offer you a glass of wine?"

"Yes, thanks, then sit down. I think I can do something with these pitas and spinach. Why don't you just go to the store?"

She stretched to pull another wine glass down from the rack hanging over the island. "I, um, I don't have a car. Not since the accident."

He chopped spinach in silence a moment, and she slid a glass of wine across the island to him. "You certainly look like you could afford a new car."

"Well, with the head injury and the meds…plus, I don't really like to leave the house anyway."

"Why not?"

Alicia sat on a barstool across from him and took a sip of her wine, letting its body coat her tongue before swallowing. "It's like this whole thing with Jude."

"Jude?"

"Judith Holloman. Apparently I knew her, socialized with her, maybe even enjoyed her company, but now I have no memory of her at all. People walk up to me and expect me to know them, or even if I do know them, they can tell me I said or did something I don't remember. I have no way of even knowing what's true—what's real. Like being told I'm happily married when the whole thing is a lie."

"Is that what happened with Meador?"

She nodded and followed her fingertip with her eyes as she ran it around the rim of her glass. "I don't think he knew what to expect when I woke up from the coma, but once he realized I didn't have any memory of his affair or asking him to move out, he tried to pretend it never happened."

"How did you find out the truth?"

"My sister Madeleine."

"Sister? For some reason I had it in my head you were an only child."

"She's my half-sister. My mother remarried after she and my father divorced. She's been in South America doing research for her doctorate. That's how I met John. She's in geology, too. He and I met when I went with her on a field study program in Peru. Now she's doing research in Colombia. Maddie flew up here right after the accident, but they had no idea when—or even if—I'd wake up. After a while, she had to go back. Evidently I had told her all about John's affair and our separation when we split up, so when I woke up and she came back a few weeks ago, she told me everything I'd forgotten. That's why it hurts so much. It's like it just happened even though it was months ago."

Mason had assembled tomato sauce and herbs with spinach, feta, and pine nuts on top of pitas arranged on a baking sheet then set them in a hot oven. "Do you know who he was sleeping with? Is it someone you know? Or might have known?"

She shrugged. "No. Some grad student. Botany. Heidi something."

"Heidi?"

"Yeah. He swears he hasn't seen her in months, but it doesn't matter. I can't even stand to look at photographs of the two of us together. I torture myself with questions. What lies did he tell me then? Did he sleep with her *this* day? Was he deceiving me in *this* picture? I was such an idiot to think that we were this happily married couple, and he was lying to me the entire time. I feel like I have no control over anything in my life, like I can't trust anyone—certainly not myself. Obviously I wasn't a very good judge of character under the best of circumstances, and now with my memory…It's enough to make me paranoid. The reality is I really don't have any control over anything. Especially now with the bras and the spoons."

"What spoons?"

"The spoons here in the kitchen. It was the morning after you were here. I went to get a spoon for my yogurt, and they were all gone. Every single one of them. I looked everywhere. There wasn't a spoon in the house. I thought I was losing it."

"Could your housekeeper have moved them?"

"No, she only comes on Wednesdays. But when I woke up the next morning—Tuesday—I get up, and they were all back."

He scowled at her then bent over to retrieve the pitas from the oven.

"They smell good," she said, but still he remained silent. "You think I'm crazy."

"What do you remember about your accident?"

"Nothing."

"The police report said alcohol was involved."

"That's what it said." She shrank under the pressure of his stare until she might as well have been ten inches tall. "So that's what you think. You think I get drunk and hide my spoons and underwear from myself."

"You don't think you were drinking and driving?"

"I haven't done something that stupid since I was a kid."

"Does anyone else have a key to your house? The maid? Your husband?"

"No. No one. I had the locks changed just recently. Plus I have an alarm. And why on earth would they hide my spoons?"

"Do you have a theory? Let's eat these before they get cold. Where are your plates? Or did they run away with the spoons?"

"Ha. Ha. To your left. If I told you my theory, you really will think I'm nuts."

"That wouldn't be hard. Go ahead."

She stalled by taking a bite. "Hmm. It's good." He ate standing up across from her, and he gave her a nod. "So, are you married?" she asked.

"No."

"Girlfriend?"

"Not yet. Now stop hedging. Tell me."

She chewed, swallowed, cleared her throat, took a sip of wine. "I...think I'm being haunted."

That he did not choke on his spinach pita she considered a testament to his self-control. He wiped his mouth with his napkin and nodded thoughtfully. "I see. So you think the house is haunted. Did someone die here?"

"No, not the house. *Me*. I think it's Mr. Holloman."

"Mr. Holloman."

"Yes. I think he's trying to communicate with me. He knows what I saw and he doesn't want me to give up on pursuing this."

"Alicia, I haven't even been able to establish that he's even missing."

"But do you know that he's alive?"

"That's beside the point. Do you really believe in ghosts?"

"I never did before, but until that night, none of these things were happening. Like I go to sleep with all the lights off, and I wake up and they're all on. And now everyday items keep getting moved."

"'Getting moved.'"

"Yes, moved. I go to look for something and it's not where I left it."

She could tell that thoughts rolled around in his head as his tongue rolled around his teeth, then he took a sip of wine. "What kind of medication are you taking?"

"Neurontin plus Ultram for pain."

Mason reached across the kitchen island and took her glass of wine. "This is what I want you to do. Stop drinking while you're taking those meds."

"Detective, I'm not imagining things."

"I'm not saying you are," he said as he poured the rest of her wine into his own glass, "but you will be a much better witness if you are clear-headed. The next time anything like this happens—anything, no matter how small—you are going to call me. Do you understand?" He grabbed her cell phone from where it lay at the end of the island and tapped his fingers across its screen.

Rolling her eyes, she asked, "What if I really have just misplaced my hairbrush or something?"

"You will call me. You have both my numbers

now. After what you've been through, you shouldn't even be alone. You need someone to take care of you, Alicia."

"Why? Because the house is haunted or because you think I'm crazy?"

Mason walked around the bar and, placing her phone on her palm, clasped her hand between both of his and captured her with his gaze. "Because you need someone who will take care of you." He lifted a fist and stroked it across her cheek. "You will call me."

"Yes," she thought she said but so quietly that even she didn't hear. That desperate, electric attraction returned, settling heavy in her belly. Damn him for making her want him to kiss her again, and damn him for not doing it! Instead, he returned to his plate, and they finished eating in silence.

"So you and your sister are close?" he asked as they began the cleaning up.

"We are now. There's quite an age gap, and of course we weren't raised together."

"You didn't go with your mother after your parents divorced?"

"For all intents and purposes, she abandoned me, and my father. I haven't even seen her in over twenty years."

"She didn't come to see you after your accident?"

"No."

"And you don't know anything about the Department of Defense?"

Alicia choked back her laughter then let it flow out. "That's quite a non sequitur! No, I don't know anything about the Department of Defense. What does it have to do with anything? Is that some kind of interrogation technique—to throw in an off-the-wall question like that?"

He shut off the water, turned from the sink, and took the dish towel from her to dry his hands. "As a matter of fact, it is. It's called a curveball."

She smiled up at him and then realized she *was* smiling, for the first time in she didn't know how long. "Did I pass the test, Detective? Do you believe me?"

Mason wrapped the towel around her waist and tugged her into the circle of his arms, then she placed her hands on his shoulders. "I told you to call me Mason," he said before dropping his mouth onto hers with a soft, lingering kiss that caused her toes to curl and made her long to deepen it, but then he released her and stepped back. "I will see you tomorrow night, unless you call me—and you *will* call me if anything unusual happens, no matter how small."

As he strode toward the door, she found herself skipping after him like a silly schoolgirl. "Wait— What? You're leaving?"

"Yes. Are you disappointed? I told you we weren't going to have sex tonight."

A flush of embarrassment washed over her. She hated to admit it, even to herself, because she was perhaps, maybe, just the tiniest bit disappointed that he didn't want to sleep with her. When he turned around, she expected his expression to be one of smug satisfaction—arrogance in astutely reading her, but she detected none of that in the slight upturn of the corners of his mouth and eyes—eyes so deep they could reach into her soul. She noticed nothing more in his countenance than a quiet confidence.

Placing a palm against her heated cheek, he leaned down and spoke in a whisper, his breath tantalizing her ear. "You don't have to worry. I *will* fuck you, Alicia. Soon."

Before she could gather her thoughts to forge a protest, he had walked out into the night, closing the door behind him. She ran her hands over her face and down her hair then returned to the kitchen and poured herself a glass of wine.

Chapter Three

As Mason drove away from the house on Lilac Lane, he wet his lips in anticipation like the cat who would soon lick the cream. An intense current of attraction connected them, and he could have kissed her for hours. No femme fatale or Mata Hari she! His first impression had been correct; Alicia was the kind of woman who needed protection, someone to take care of her, and he wanted that role. He hadn't had that kind of relationship in far too long, and the void stabbed him like a knife in his side.

The confetti pieces of her past reassembled to create a perfect mosaic of a girl who had grown up needing only to be wanted and loved by her parents, seeking that out in a weak-willed father-figure of a husband who had no idea what it would take for her to be fulfilled. Hell, *she* didn't even realize what she needed. But Mason did, and he would enjoy giving it to her. She would learn that sometimes *not* being in control was the most beautiful thing in the world.

Unfortunately, two sizeable barriers lay in the way of their progress: the mystery surrounding the disappearance of her neighbor, and the possibility of her drug and alcohol fueled—or injury induced—delusions. No matter how many answers he got from her, he always wound up with more questions. The brick walls he had run into with Holloman were one thing, but something about Alicia's accident didn't add up. And why did the name "Heidi" resonate with him?

"What the hell?" he said aloud as he craned his neck watching John Meador drive past him toward Alicia's house, and Meador turned his head to stare back at him. What reason did *he* have to be going over there at this time of night?

The next day when Mason arrived at the sheriff's station, he pulled up Alicia's accident report again. No matter how many times he read it over, he caught nothing new in the facts, and yet something nagged at him. He brought up the news article photos again. Maybe if he saw the car himself—that is, if it hadn't already been smashed into scrap.

He found the number of the tow service they usually used. "Yeah, this is Detective Mason Crawley," he said to the woman who answered when he called. "I wanted to see if you had a vehicle there." He read her the last six digits of the VIN, and she placed him on hold.

After a clank and a thunk, a man's voice came through. "Hey, you calling about that BMW?"

"Yes, it was pulled from a lake a few months back."

"Man, you called just in time. We just got that title

in today. It would be going to the scrap yard tomorrow."

"Don't do anything with it. I'm on my way."

When he arrived at the tow yard, the car appeared much the same as it had in the pictures, although the smell that erupted when he opened the driver's side door bore witness that it had been waterlogged then left to sit in the sun for nearly three months. Mason examined the car inside and out for ten minutes, searching for anything that seemed off, but other than the smell and the damage to the front end, the car was in nearly perfect condition. As he slammed the driver's door, it struck him, and he opened it again. The airbag.

"Hey, Mel," he called out to the owner. "Any reason why the airbag wouldn't have deployed?" Mel hopped over, and Mason stepped aside to let the man take a look. "Is it defective or something?"

Mel fiddled around for a few minutes then stood, shaking his head, his hands on his hips. "Nope. Looks fine to me."

"So why wouldn't it deploy if the driver drove off the road and into a lake?"

"Had to be going pretty damn slow, if you ask me. More likely rolled into the lake."

"Rolled?" If Alicia had slowly rolled into the lake, then how in holy hell had she sustained the head injuries that put her in a coma for two months?

Alicia wanted to kick herself for the butterflies fluttering through her, the rush of excitement that coursed through her every time she thought of his raspy words in her ear, the way the memory shot a spark straight to that spot between her legs. What was she? Some kind of horny coed? She was an adult woman, for Christ's sake! How dare he speak to her that way! Was this some sort of macho-cop bullshit or something? And *kiss* her!

Then she smiled. *Mmm*...she liked the way he kissed her. And the way he spoke to her—the threat or the promise of what was to come. Even the word *come* made her giggle. And she covered her mouth with her hands. Maybe she wasn't such an adult after all.

The trademark tones of Skype beckoned from the computer nook, and she skipped over in anticipation of seeing her sister.

"Hey! How are you?" Alicia asked as she sat before the screen.

"Doing great. How 'bout you?" Maddie's image peeled across the screen in stop-gap animation.

"I'm better. Still a lot of headaches."

"Well, you sound better and—Wait...Are you smiling?"

Alicia could do little more than blush and damn webcams. Maddie's comment only served to broaden her grin, and she rolled her eyes to the ceiling.

"C'mon. What's going on, Alish?"

"I, uh, I might have met someone."

"Holy shit. You actually left the house? What do you mean you 'might have'? Either you did or you didn't."

"Well, yeah, I met someone, but I don't know. It's complicated."

"What relationship isn't?"

"Yeah, but he's a cop."

"A cop! Oh, my God, Alicia! Run! What are you thinking?"

"I know! But he's not like a *cop* cop. He's a detective."

"You've been popped more often than bubble wrap."

"Oh, c'mon. That's—that's a terrible metaphor! And that was a long time ago."

Maddie laughed. "I should have suspected there was an ulterior motive to your misspent youth."

"Not hardly."

"Hey, I'm just glad to see you smiling again. So what's his name? How did you meet him?"

"His name's Mason, and he...I...he came out, well, it doesn't matter. I suspected something was going on with the neighbors, but it's probably nothing. Anyway, he's coming over tonight, and I need to jump in the shower."

After chatting a few minutes longer about Maddie's activities in Colombia, they signed off and Alicia stared at the blank screen, tapping on the mouse. She had no idea what time Mason would show up, and now she almost regretted not having had an excuse to call him all day; but, alas, so far nothing had gone missing. Would he want to eat again? She still lacked the mettle to face the world at large, and she wondered if he would be amenable to ordering in.

As she walked toward the kitchen, Alicia heard voices floating over from across the lake. She never had opened the blinds after Mason closed them the night before, but she had left one of the French doors open after coming in that afternoon. She flicked off the switch to leave her in darkness and stepped silently into the doorway to listen.

Jude's voice rose in anger, but once again Alicia couldn't make out the words. Then a male voice shouted back. Had Daniel Holloman returned after all? That would certainly cement Mason's opinion of her as a delusional fool.

Alicia slipped through the French door into the night and out onto the terrace then made her way down to the edge of the water. She could see them in silhouette now, both standing in Jude's kitchen and speaking in loud, agitated tones, but she still couldn't understand what they were saying. She squinted as if it might help her hear better. The house lay only thirty yards from her across the water, but to get to it from the other side, one would have to go clear around the lake on the next street. If she had a car, it would take only a few minutes, but she didn't. On foot, it might take half an hour. She had no choice but to cross the lake.

They usually used a small three-seater paddle boat to go around the lake, but the splashing would make too much noise. Instead she would have to use one of their single-person kayaks. She glanced down at her bare feet then back up at the arguing couple. No, she had to find out if Jude's husband really was alive, and she didn't want to waste time looking for shoes.

Alicia carefully navigated the slick muddy slope over to where the kayaks were tied upside down. The rattles and burps of the crickets and frogs obscured the voices further. As quietly as possible, she freed one of kayaks and waded with it into the water until she was knee deep, the cool water sending a chilly quiver up her spine as her feet sank into the slimy mud that gripped her toes like thick glue. If Holloman really was alive, she hoped he had killed all the snakes.

Once she had pulled herself into the kayak, she cut the oar into the water with her jaw clenched, as if that might help quiet the sound of the ripples, and steered slightly south of Jude's house so the couple wouldn't notice her approach. For a while she couldn't see them, but as she neared the opposite shore, their volume increased. No, that wasn't Daniel Holloman. She knew that voice well. John. What was he doing over there? How on earth would he be involved in the disappearance of Jude's husband? The next thing to come to mind, of course, was that he and Jude were having an affair too.

"How can you not know when he'll be back?" John was yelling.

Alicia tugged the kayak up a few feet then slunk bent over across the deck until she stood just outside the kitchen window, her heart pounding against her sternum and her breath huffing out in rapid puffs.

"I never know when he'll be back," Jude said. "It doesn't work that way."

"He's your husband. Isn't he?"

"You're one to talk. I don't think you'll be winning any marriage of the year awards."

"What did you say to Alicia?"

Alicia flinched at the sound of her name on her husband's tongue.

"About what?"

"What the hell do you think? About Danny!"

"I told you, I didn't tell her anything. I just hoped she might remember me."

"Stay away from her. Do you hear? I don't want you talking to her."

A chill from nowhere rushed through Alicia, choking her with the sensation of falling while asleep, and a thundering paralysis struck her like a bolt of lightning. The blinding pain pulsating in her skull rendered her deaf and blind and incapable of any motion beyond grasping her head in her hands as an ethereal, high-pitched note reverberated through her brain. She remained standing in place but disconnected from her present surroundings, aware only of the ringing in her ears and the nausea rising in her throat.

"I want you to stay away from her!" John's harsh words shook Alicia from her torpor, although she was still acutely aware of the pulse striking against her temple.

"I don't see why that's any of your business!"

"She's my wife!"

"Not for long! It's time for you to go," Jude said and headed toward the door.

As Alicia realized they would find her the moment they stepped out of the house, her breaths and heart rate increased, and she staggered back down to the kayak. She pushed it into the water just as a car door slammed behind her, and she clambered over the side. Half in and half out, she struggled with the oar to get across, then the kayak capsized, taking her with it and covering her under the water.

Panic filled her faster than the water, like a black

liquid overwhelming every particle of her physical being before invading her mind. Then she drifted and sank, lower and lower, floating yet sinking, her waterlogged sweater an anchor dragging her down. In this hypnogogic state, minuscule flecks of memory intruded on the siren's lullaby, the song enticing her to give in to the allure of letting go of all the pain, the heartache, the worry. Calling out, *Let go.* Fall back into the welcoming embrace of death with no fear of pain, no risk of betrayal. *Yes. Take me.*

As she drew near to that infinite darkness, a hard yank on her hair pulled her back into semi-consciousness. The cold night air swept over her wet skin, and she gasped and coughed and fought her attacker—her rescuer—before she surrendered and collapsed in his arms.

Alicia had no idea how much time had passed when she lifted one eyelid just enough to see through her lashes. After allowing her senses to absorb the environment for a few moments—the smell of hot wax; the dense, humid air; the sound of running water; the cold, hard floor; the warm, dry swaddling—she realized she lay wrapped in a blanket on her bathroom floor with the tub being filled with water. She closed her eye again.

A murmur of protest escaped her lips when the blanket jerked free, her limbs resisting like lead abetted by gravity as hard arms lifted her from the floor. Then she slid once again into water, hot this time and redolent with her favorite scents, until only the top of her face remained above the surface and bubbles tickled her cheeks. Sooner than she would have liked, two rough hands grabbed her from under her arms and pulled her up into a sitting position. She leaned forward against her bent knees, her arms wrapped around her calves in some pretense of modesty. She didn't need to hear his voice to know the hands belonged to Mason.

"What the hell were you doing out there?"

She had expected anger or outrage, for him to yell at her, but he spoke softly, gently, in that same deep, resonating timbre he had used when he said he was going to kiss her. When she opened her eyes, the lights were all off, and she sat surrounded by candles in a tub of bubbles with Mason balanced on the edge behind her. She glanced over her shoulder at him just as he began to run a wet washcloth down her back. A towel tied at his waist covered his hips and thighs, and she recognized the smell of her shower gel on his skin.

"Were you trying to kill yourself?" he asked, meeting her eyes for a moment before refocusing on his task.

Alicia closed her eyes again and basked under his ministrations. "No, I heard arguing. Jude and a man. It was John."

When she said the name, Mason halted his progress down her back. After a moment, he lifted her hair from her shoulders and, first dunking the cloth in the tub, squeezed the water out over the back of her neck. He did that a few more times before setting the washcloth aside and massaging her neck and shoulders with such finesse she wanted to purr like a kitten.

"Here. Lie back," he murmured. She opened her eyes but didn't move. "I've already seen you, Alicia, and I'll be seeing much more of you soon."

His confidence sparked both an urge to resist and a tingle between her legs. Still she hesitated before leaning back, thankful that the bubbles offered some coverage even while acknowledging to herself the inanity of her prudishness since Mason had obviously undressed her before unceremoniously submerging her in the tub. "And where are your clothes?" she asked.

He came around and knelt at her side, his dark blue eyes driving into hers as he rubbed the washcloth around her face and neck. "You were supposed to call me," he said, his volume still low but with an edge to his tone.

"I…I forgot." Oddly enough, she truly had. The idea hadn't even crossed her mind, despite only moments before having wished she'd had an excuse to call him. All she had thought of was getting over there to learn the truth.

"You could have drowned."

She forced her gaze down, unable to bear the intensity of his stare—especially knowing how near she had been to succumbing to the temptation, so close she could almost taste it. Of being absorbed into nothingness like sinking into quicksand, the sandman of eternal sleep.

Mason grabbed her chin and forced her to face him. "You disobeyed me."

She tried to jerk free but he held firm. The audacity! To think he had the right to issue orders to her and reprimand her when she *disobeyed*! Alicia clenched her teeth and scowled. "I can take the kayak out any time I damn well please," she said tersely.

"We will discuss rules for nighttime kayaking another time—that's beside the point. You were supposed to call me if anything out of the ordinary happened, if a single spoon were out of place. Do you recall agreeing to that last night?"

She looked down, and he released her chin. "Yes."

"I told you, you need someone taking care of you, and obviously I am right. What were you thinking?"

"I-I heard voices, arguing. I thought Jude's husband might be back, and I wanted to find out."

"And you didn't call me because…"

"I don't know why—I didn't think. I just acted. I just wanted to find out what was going on."

"I have to be able to trust you, too, Alicia. I have to know that you will obey my orders so I can keep you safe. Your first instinct should be to call me. Understand?"

She nodded without conviction and, glancing around, noticed the bubbles were disappearing. "Can I get out now?"

"No. Before you almost managed to kill yourself, did you hear what they were saying? Why was Meador over there? What were they arguing about?"

"It sounded like he was confronting her about her husband's disappearance, that it was suspicious for her not to know when he'd be back. And he told her to stay away from me. Maybe he thinks she did kill him. I guess he was trying to protect me."

"What was he doing here last night?"

"Who?"

"Meador."

She turned her face up to him and narrowed her eyes. "What are you talking about? I haven't seen him since Sunday night."

He forced himself up and loomed over her so she had to crane her neck to look at him. "I know that's not true. I passed him on the street as I was leaving last night."

"Well, he didn't come here."

"You have to trust me, Alicia. Tell me the truth." His voice had picked up volume and bounced off the tile enclosure.

"I *am* telling you the truth. He wasn't here. I *do* trust you."

"Are you willing to prove it?"

She didn't answer. Instead, she dropped her head to face forward, a dozen thoughts buzzing around in her mind.

Mason grabbed a fresh, oversized towel and held it up in front of him near the edge of the tub. "Stand up."

"I can dry off myself."

"Stand up."

With a huff, she hoisted herself up at a twisted angle so she rose with her back to him. He wrapped the towel around her then methodically patted it down to her feet then back up again before twisting it together under her arms. Then he turned her around, took her hand, and tugged her toward the bedroom.

"Come with me."

Mason had her sit on the bed and told her not to move as he disappeared into the living room, leaving her alone with the impulse to get up and get dressed just to defy him, but she didn't. He returned a few minutes later with a set of handcuffs hanging from his index finger. She stared at the steel rings and then up into his cold, unreadable eyes, and the blood rushed out of her face and tightened around her throat.

"Are you arresting me?"

A brief quiver at the corner of his mouth made her wonder if he were trying to suppress a smile. "No, my pet. You say you trust me. Do you trust me enough to let me put these on you? To leave yourself open and helpless to anything and everything I have planned for you?"

Her eyes widened and her mouth opened, but no words came out. She didn't know what to say. A tiny voice in her head reminded her of everything she'd been taught to think about women being strong and independent. Everything she had believed about herself bristled at the idea of-of-of *submitting* to his will. She was a feminist, for God's sake. But the words "leave yourself open and helpless to anything and everything I have planned for you" had reached between her legs as if he had actually touched her there. Her arousal shamed her, and the blood returned to bloom in her cheeks even as it rushed to her womb.

"Do you trust me to stop at any time—if you ever feel uncomfortable—when you say the word?" When she still said nothing, he added, "You remember the word?"

She nodded. *Apple,* she said to herself.

"What is your answer, Alicia?"

She glanced back at the cuffs then up into his eyes. What the hell was she doing?

"Yes."

"Extend your arms," he said, and she obeyed. A good beginning. He affixed the cuffs just enough so her tiny hands couldn't slip through.

Mason didn't like using his police-issue cuffs, but he hadn't intended on taking their relationship to this level tonight. Unfortunately, she had upped the ante by nearly killing herself, and now he had no choice but to take control.

Once the cuffs were secure, the chocolate eyes fringed with black lashes rolled up to meet his as if awaiting further instruction. "Good girl," he said, brushing his knuckles across her jawline. "Now there is a difference between feeling discomfort and uncomfortable. If you're at an awkward angle or your hand is getting numb, just say so. Your safety word is if you find the activity itself uncomfortable to the point that you want me to stop immediately. Understood?" She nodded.

Although he maintained the façade of self-assurance, he himself lacked the confidence he usually had in such a scene. They had not discussed any ground rules beforehand, had established no hard limits. He had nothing with him except that blasted pair of police handcuffs, but she couldn't know that—she had to have absolute faith in him and his strength and capabilities, believe she could rely on him to take care of her. He would just play it by ear, take it slow, which—considering he hadn't had a sub in over a year—was probably the way to begin regardless.

"Now," he told her, "take off the towel and lie on your stomach across the bed with your head and arms on the edge."

"But my hands are cuffed."

"You'll manage. I'll be right back." Mason returned to the master bath and rifled through the cabinets until he found body oil. Not massage oil, but it would have to do. He returned to find Alicia had followed his instructions, more or less. Instead of the towel, she had covered herself with the sheet, and she lay horizontal across the bed resting her head between her restrained arms.

Standing at her head, Mason pulled the sheet down slowly, teasing her by running it down to the small of her back, and she tensed until he released it, leaving her covered from the hips down. He took the oil and warmed it between his hands before leaning over and massaging and kneading the muscles of her neck, shoulders, and back, working methodically up and down, reaching slightly lower each time toward the edge of the sheet, and he began to harden with each pass of his hands over her silky bare skin.

Alicia moaned under the pressure of his thumbs and the heels of his hands, increasing his arousal, twitching against the towel still around his waist.

"Mmmm…" she groaned. "If I'd known this was what you had planned, I would have jumped into these handcuffs."

He smiled. "I've only just begun." He stepped back, and she whined in protest. After walking around to the other side of the bed, he dropped the towel, his hard length springing free. He pulled the sheet off of her bottom half in one swift motion, and she squealed, pulling her legs tight together. He stood enthralled by her beauty there, stretched out before him across the bed with the steel cuffs encircling her wrists. She strained to see behind her, but he had stopped just outside her field of vision. Then he knelt upon the bed and moved toward her, straddling her legs with his calves resting on either side of her thighs.

Gathering more oil between his hands, Mason resumed the massage from her waist to the small of her back then continued down to her soft ass and squeezed both cool cheeks in his large hands until finally she stopped resisting and relaxed against the bed with a sigh. He rubbed the oil in from the bottom of her back to the top of her thighs and then up again. Her muscles loosened under his palms and her breathing slowed. He tilted his head to see her eyes were closed and her lips formed into a slight smile.

"You disobeyed me, my pet," he said, his gravelly words just loud enough so she would hear. "Disobedience must be punished." He raised his hand and brought it down on her right cheek with a crisp, echoing slap.

She screeched and her entire body tensed. "Hey!" she said as she craned her neck to meet his eyes, but a tickle trebled the syllable. Then she began to laugh, which had to be the last response he would have expected. Outrage. Indignation from a spoiled princess. Even crying as the culmination of days— *months*—of crisis. Fortunately, her reaction had done nothing to diminish his erection, and his cock ached to delve into that crevice.

As he rubbed the red mark on her smooth skin, his brows drew together, and he did his best to maintain a level, serious tone. "Do you find something amusing, my pet?"

"You spanked me!"

"You disobeyed me." He slapped the other cheek, which set off her laughter again. "Does spanking always make you laugh?" he asked as he rubbed the body oil into both of her cheeks.

"Um, I don't know. I've never been spanked before."

"Even when you were naughty when you were a little girl?"

"Never."

"Did you like it when I spanked you?"

"I...no."

He spanked her again, harder this time, but before she had a chance to laugh, he slid two fingers down her slit and into her, eliciting a satisfying gasp. "I think you did like it," he said as he pumped his fingers in and out. "Feel how wet you are." She was wet, too, and the more he rolled his fingers inside of her, the wetter she became, and her murmured moans increased with her breaths as she wiggled against his hand. After too many months of abstinence, he wanted to lift her hips up now and plunge in, but for their first night together, he had to demonstrate complete control. He pulled out his fingers then circled her clit before running them up her slit and away.

"Why'd you stop?" she asked on a hot breath. He scooted up and leaned forward, the head of his cock nudging between her cheeks, and she flinched. "Is that your..."

"My cock?"

"Oh, God. You're not planning on going anal. Are you?"

Now he laughed at the sound of sheer terror in her

voice. "C'mon. Roll over." He helped her turn over onto her back, her cuffed hands hanging off the bed over her head. Her nipples hardened under his appreciative gaze. He caught her glance to where his cock hovered over her tummy before quickly looking up at his face, and he smiled at the blush rising in her cheeks. "Do you like what you see?" He certainly enjoyed the beauty lying before him, at his mercy, as her breasts rose and fell under his appraising stare. "I certainly do."

Mason came down over her, supporting himself with his arms beside her head, and gazed into her eager eyes, full of wonder for what might happen next. He combed his fingers through her hair, still wet from the bath, then covered her mouth with his. She returned his kiss with fervor, lifting her head from the bed as if it might bring their tongues deeper as the chain clinked against the cuffs. He pushed himself up and admired her swollen lips.

Mason grabbed the oil and poured some on his palm before closing the bottle and tossing it back on the bed. He warmed the oil between his hands then worked his way from her upper arms to her collarbones, down her chest and began massaging her breasts. He leaned over and suckled one and then the other nipple as she mewed her approval. His cock throbbed against her belly, its tightness demanding release.

"Where are your condoms?" he asked.

"What? I don't have any. I haven't been with anyone but my husband since we got married."

Shit. He hadn't brought any either. Once again, he would come across as an amateur, not knowing what he was doing. How could she have faith or trust in someone who arrived at a scene so ill-prepared? He had never allowed himself to be this spontaneous, to jump in without discussing the unsavory topics of pregnancy or test results beforehand. He knew he was clean—he always made sure of that. He didn't doubt Alicia had been faithful to Meador, but God knew how many co-eds that jackass had banged or what he might have exposed Alicia to. But, damn it, Mason wanted to bury himself deep inside of her.

"I..." she began. "It's all right. You can go ahead. I won't get pregnant."

Ha! Her directive settled everything. She had to learn *he* had control. *He* was in charge. With his resurgent confidence, he hopped off the bed and grabbed the keys from the dresser. "You have been disobedient," he said. "Until I am sure I can trust you, I'm not going to take any chances." He unlocked the cuff to release one wrist as she watched him with a frown of mingled confusion and disappointment.

"So we're done?" she asked.

"Nope. Slide up here. Have you ever been bound before, with ropes or cuffs?" She shook her head, and he helped her up to the top of the bed resting her head on the pillows. After looping the cuffs around the headboard and reattaching her wrist, he adjusted the pillows under her wrists, head, and neck. "Comfortable?" She nodded. He grabbed her hair with force and pulled her head back then thrust his tongue deep into her mouth, kissing her ravenously. She reciprocated and sucked his tongue, sending a jolt straight to his groin.

As Mason kissed her, his hand traced down her

side then straight to her core, dipping between her folds and easily slipping two fingers inside of her. He began a methodical rhythm, sliding out and over her clit then back in again, repeating this as she raised her hips up, keeping with his tempo.

He broke the kiss, leaving them both panting, and pulled his hand away. "I am still going to fuck you, but since you haven't shown me I can trust you, I'll just have to come in this beautiful mouth of yours." Mason couldn't suppress the grin that spread across his face at the sight of her wide, bulging eyes.

"No, you can't!"

"Oh, yes, I assure you, I most definitely can—and I will. And you are not in any position to deny me." He rolled over her and between her legs, positioning the head of his cock at her entrance. God, it would take all his self-control to pull out in time.

"No, I mean, I don't want you to. I don't do that."

"Well, you're about to."

Her wrists strained against the cuffs. "Please, Mason, please don't make me."

To be certain, he said, "Alicia, do you remember the word?"

She stared at him in silence as they breathed in rapid synchronicity for several excruciating moments. "Yes."

As the syllable still hung in the air, he drove into her, filling her to the hilt in one motion and forcing the air from her lungs as she cried out her delight.

Alicia felt wild—outside of herself. Out of control.

She *was* out of control. He was in control. Mason. She had given him complete control, and he rewarded her with pleasure beyond her imagination. A woman's voice cried out and echoed throughout the room. Alicia opened her eyes then realized it was her own cries of ecstasy. She knew it had been a while since she and John had slept together, but she didn't remember it ever turning her inside out like this. As he pounded into her, she wrapped her legs around his waist to bring him deeper, which might prove impossible. He filled her completely. Never before had a man fit her so perfectly.

Mason braced himself on the headboard, as if he instinctively knew she wanted him to go harder, deeper. "God, you're so tight," he croaked out.

Then she worried. The insecurity returned, of something being wrong with her. Was she *too* tight? He had such a pained expression on his face. "Am I too tight?"

He breathed out a laugh. "No, my pet. You are perfect. I wish I could fuck you all night."

His use of the profanity both embarrassed and aroused her, which embarrassed her even more. Then she glimpsed the cuffs on her wrists, gleaming like silver bracelets, and her womb flipped at the sight of her helplessness. He lengthened and hardened inside of her, and she thought he might be nearing his climax, so she raised her hips to meet him. He couldn't *really* intend to pull out now and come in her mouth. Why hadn't she said apple? As the waves of sensation poured over her, the realization stunned her. She must *want* it. Each time she thought of him putting him*self* in her mouth as she lay helpless, heat flared between her legs and a sharp sizzle ran over her tiny nub until she began to think she would soon come herself.

Mason must have sensed it, too, because he reached one hand down to stroke her clit, and that combined with his continued thrusts, brought her teetering on the edge. "Ah, my pet. Do you want to come for me?" She arched her back, but when she didn't answer, he stopped. "I asked you a question. Do you want to come for me?" He stopped pushing into her then, before barely running a finger over that most sensitive pearl of flesh.

"Oh, God, yes," she cried out.

"No, I'm not God. Say, 'May I please come for you, Sir?'"

She was ready to scream the Gettysburg Address if necessary. "May I please come for you, Sir?"

Mason ground into her deep and fast as he circled her clit with the perfect amount of pressure to send her soaring and screaming and coming harder than she could remember ever having come before. She knew that she flopped and thrashed against the bed like Regan in *The Exorcist* as the cuffs chafed her skin, but as the lights exploded behind her eyelids, nothing could have mattered to her less. Only in the aftershocks of her climax did she realize Mason had, indeed, withdrawn from her.

"And now, my pet," he said as he moved up to straddle her chest. "My turn."

Once staring his *manhood* eye to eye, the panic set in. "Mason, you don't really want me to..."

"Suck my cock?"

She cringed, and the cuffs clanged together. "But

you've been inside of me. It'll taste like…"

"Your pussy?"

"Ugh. I hate that term."

"Your c—"

"Don't even say it!"

He huffed out a sigh. "It's your body. We'll call it whatever you like. What do you call it?"

"I don't know. *Down there*."

Mason started laughing, which shook the bed and caused his…*thing* to bob up and down in front of her face. "I can't call it 'down there.' Too much like 'down under'—Australia or something. You can decide later. But this is my *cock* and you will suck it—now." She squeezed her eyes closed tight and parted her lips a fraction. He took her chin in his hand and pulled her mouth open.

Then, he had done it. His *cock* was in her mouth! He rocked his hips so that the silk-covered-steel stroked from the tip of her tongue to her tonsils, the ridge of its head skidding across the roof of her mouth. And never before had she experienced anything so erotic and exotic. That this aroused her shocked her even more, and her own hips moved against the bed in time with his, seemingly of their own accord. Her tongue swirled around this welcome invader, provoking an appreciative groan from his hard, heavy breathing, which struck her to the core. Would it be possible for *her* to come while performing this act on *him*? Scrumptious. Truly scrumptious. Those were the only words she could think of to describe her new-found guilty pleasure. Like the song from *Mary Poppins*. No. *Chitty, Chitty, Bang, Bang. That's it! Oh, God.* She was definitely going to hell for equating fellatio with a children's song! But he did seem to be rocking to that rhythm.

Then she recalled his directive and began to suck on his shaft—hard. The way he moaned, she thought she might have sucked too hard, but then he lengthened, tightened, and quivered in her mouth as warm, tangy liquid poured down her throat. Delighted with her success, she swallowed and sucked again until certain she had gotten every last drop, and he pulled out and flopped beside her on the bed.

And then, she laughed.

She laughed because never before had she felt so clean and so dirty, so free yet so controlled. In all the days of her misspent youth, never had she allowed herself the pleasure of such perceived degradation. She opened her eyes, looking herself over, bound and bare before this man she hardly knew, then she rolled her head to face him as her giggling continued, and not just because the irony of *bang, bang* had finally hit her. Mason lay there watching her, one arm thrown across his forehead, his chest still rising and falling rapidly, and a smile twitching at the corners of his mouth.

"Did you find my orgasm amusing, my pet?"

"No, I…I didn't think I would enjoy it."

"Even though I tasted like Australia?"

"Australia?" He flicked his eyes *down there*, and she blushed. "Oh. I didn't even think about it. I mean it really, well, it really…turned me on."

Mason rolled onto his side and ran his hand down her tummy and over her clit, causing her breath to catch, before trailing over her slit. "God, you are wet," he said as he pushed his fingers into her. She moaned and her eyes closed again. "Where's your vibrator?" he asked.

"Pfft. With the condoms."

"What do you mean?"

"I don't have one."

"C'mon. Really?"

"I've never even used one."

"Never?" He sounded legitimately surprised. "Well, you have plenty to look forward to then. In the meantime…" and he worked his magic fingers in and out and around until she screamed and saw fireworks and her womb jumped for joy.

Chapter Four

Mason didn't want to leave—he hated it, in fact—but he had strict rules when taking on a new sub. The first, well, he had already broken by going forward without any preparations. No discussions, no ground rules, not even any condoms. He hadn't planned for any of that to happen that night. He had gone in half-cocked, so to speak, with nothing but a hard-on, handcuffs, and a safety word. He refused to break the next one—emotional detachment—although for him that ship had long since sailed. Nevertheless, he knew the problems that could arise from indulging in emotional intimacy prematurely—if ever—before knowing if they were compatible on other levels and an understanding had been reached. So he considered it a hard rule not to spend the night with a sub until they had an agreement, a rule he had never wanted to bend before this evening.

Alicia, on the other hand, accepted his departure without the slightest hint of disappointment. He had pulled the covers up to her neck before unlocking the handcuffs, kissing and caressing the impressions they had made on her wrists. He curled his arms around her body, limp from the kind of exhaustion that could only come from intense sexual satisfaction, and held her in tender aftercare as she dozed off. After a while, she stretched and smiled and rolled around in his arms to face him. He let his fingertips trail lightly from her forehead to her jaw then kissed her perfect pink lips.

"How do you feel?" he asked.

"Mmmm...hungry. You?"

"Yes, but I can't stay." He waited a moment for her to object or for a petulant scowl to cut between her chocolate eyes, but when her sleepy smile remained unfazed, he went on. "There's something I have to follow up on tonight for a case I'm working on." Not that she'd asked for an explanation. "Did you ever get any food in this damn place?"

She pulled out of his embrace and yawned, covering her mouth with the back of her hand. "I'll order in. I'm kind of in the mood for pizza." As she sat up, she adjusted the sheet to cover herself then rubbed her wrists.

He propped his head on his elbow with his fist. "Alicia, are you OK with everything? With what we did tonight?" From that angle, he could only glimpse the side of her cheek, but he thought he saw her blush. He liked making her blush.

"Yes. I..." She glanced over her shoulder at him. "I hope I did it all right."

Mason fell back against the pillow laughing. "Oh, God, yes. Better than all right. You said you never did that? Not even with your husband?"

"Well, yes, of…" She turned away and released an aggravated sigh. "Look. Can we make a deal *never* to discuss my sex life with my husband? Ever?"

Mason stroked his fingers down her spine. "Absolutely."

They hadn't said much after that. Mason's clothes were dry enough to put on but held onto the stench of the lake. When he'd rushed out and seen Alicia face-down in the lake, he didn't want to waste any more time than it took to kick off his shoes and remove his holster before jumping in and carrying her out. As he dressed, he heard Alicia in the other room ordering her pizza. Then she walked back into the bedroom in that same silky robe she'd worn the night before, but now instead of tears, a glow adorned her face—the allure of a woman transformed. *He* had done that, he knew, feeling more of a sense of accomplishment than arrogance. He hoped he could make it last for more than just one night.

"Pizza's on its way," she said.

"You don't exactly eat a healthy diet."

"What? It's all the basic food groups. Meat, cheese is dairy, tomato sauce and mushrooms for vegetables."

"There's no fruit."

"Technically, tomatoes are fruit. Anyway I'll have a glass of wine—grapes!"

"I told you, no more wine." He walked past her toward the living room and wedged his feet into his shoes without socks. "I'll come back tomorrow night," he said when she joined him, "unless something happens and you call me. And I mean *any*thing. Do you understand?"

"Yes, sir," she replied with a mock salute.

"I'm serious, Alicia. I expect you to obey me on this."

With her eyes now turned downward, she nodded. Much better. "Yes, Mason. I understand. I will call you."

Grateful that he'd tossed the keys on the kitchen island before jumping into the lake, he grabbed them and headed for the door. Just as he twisted the doorknob, he stopped and turned to face her where she stood not a foot behind him. "Almost forgot. There was something I wanted to ask you. When I pulled you from the lake, you kept repeating a name. Heidi Doucet. Who is that?"

Alicia turned red then white before his eyes. "That was my husband's mistress."

That provided Mason with even more incentive for his plans for the rest of the night, after a quick stop at his place to change. He hadn't lied to Alicia when he'd told her he wanted to follow up on a case he was working on. He just didn't say it was her case. From the moment she had told him Meador had been arguing with Judith Holloman, Mason had decided he would be paying that particular *doctor* a house call.

John Meador had had the good fortune of finding a colleague going on sabbatical, and so the bastard had fallen into rather plush, furnished accommodations not far from campus. Mason cut his headlights as he drove closer to the address so as not to alert Meador of his approach. He turned off the engine and waited. Ten o'clock. Late, perhaps, for some, but most of the lights were on inside the house, and Mason caught a shadow occasionally darken the curtains.

Mason closed his car door with as little noise as possible, walked up to the house in silence, then banged on the door with a resounding force. He caught the flutter of curtains from the corner of his eye, but no one came to the door. He hit on it again.

"Meador, I know you're in there. Open the door." Then with the volume he knew would always do the trick, lest the neighbors became suspicious, he said, "This is the police!"

In an instant, the locks were clicking, and the door fell open onto the lanky, red-faced man. "What are you doing here, Crawley? Do you know what time it is?"

Mason shoved past him into the cluttered living room filled with good furniture, although worn with age, and overflowing with books and papers. The house reeked with the aroma of an old bookstore. "I have a watch, Meador. That's not why I'm here."

Meador's shoulders drooped and he closed the door in resignation. "Then what is it that could not wait until morning? Is there news about Danny Holloman?"

"That's actually what I came to ask you. What were you doing over at the Holloman place tonight? Don't bother denying it. You were heard arguing with Judith Holloman."

Meador's eyes flickered rapidly, as if searching for a quick response. "I'm concerned about Alicia," he said finally. "I am afraid of what that woman might do to her."

"I thought you didn't believe Alicia's story, that you didn't think anything had happened to Daniel."

"I don't."

"So you don't think Mrs. Holloman killed her husband?"

Meador pulled back his shoulders and straightened to his full height. "No, of course not."

"Then why would Alicia be in danger?"

"I don't mean in any *physical* danger. Alicia is in a very precarious mental state right now. The last thing she needs is someone she doesn't even remember pressuring her. That's probably why she started having the delusions about the Hollomans in the first place. Just being across the lake from them, living in that house, alone. She needs someone there to take care of her."

Agreeing with Meador struck Mason like a punch to the gut. He had hated this guy on sight—even before he knew how he'd hurt Alicia. Even before he had fucked the man's wife.

"I've been seeing your car on Lilac Lane recently, Detective," Meador said, arching his brow. "Something I should know about my *wife*?"

"I've had a few follow-up questions. And she wants me to keep her informed if anything comes up." Mason wondered how much time Meador had spent on Lilac Lane over the last two nights, if he might suspect something was going on between him and Alicia. He hoped he did. "What can you tell me about Heidi Doucet?"

Meador's face turned crimson, and his Adam's apple throbbed as he swallowed. "Yes, I'm not proud of it. I had an affair—a *brief* affair—with Heidi Doucet."

"Are you seeing her now?"

"No."

"Even though you and Alicia are separated?"

Meador raised his eyebrows at the familiarity with which Mason had used her name. "No, I am not. I still hope Alicia and I can work things out."

Mason sniffed his contempt.

"Whatever you may think of *me*, Detective, I love my wife. I made a mistake, one which I will regret for the rest of my life."

"How can I reach Miss Doucet?"

"I have no idea. As I told Alicia, I broke it off with her months ago, and I haven't seen her or spoken to her since. Are we about done here?"

"Just one more thing. What can you tell me about Alicia's accident?"

Oddly, Meador colored and gulped, reacting in the same manner as when Mason had said the name of his mistress—a *tell*. Guilt?

"Nothing, I'm afraid. I wasn't there."

"Don't you find it odd that her airbag never deployed? She couldn't have been going very fast."

Meador's entire body stiffened. "I wasn't aware of that. Perhaps she fell asleep at the wheel."

"And sustained such serious head injuries?"

"Maybe she wasn't wearing her seatbelt and hit her head on the roof. As she made so abundantly clear, I am not a *medical* doctor."

"They said she'd been drinking."

Meador braced his hands on his hips and sighed, staring off beyond Mason. "I feel responsible for the whole thing. You have no idea how much I have suffered because of it. You see, we had been fighting—about Heidi—even though I told her it was over. She'd been drinking. I begged her not to go, but she wouldn't listen."

"What was she doing out by the campus lakes? That's quite a distance from your house."

Meador hesitated before answering. "She said she was going to go confront Heidi—she wanted to face 'that little whore' herself."

Little whore? That didn't sound like something Alicia would say, but maybe, with the incentive of jealousy and the courage of cocktails. "Did she confront her?"

"I don't know if she made it that far or if she had the accident on her way."

"You never heard from Miss Doucet? You didn't try to contact her to find out?"

"No, and with my wife in a coma, you can see why that would not have been uppermost on my mind. Now is there anything else?"

"Not at this time. For now, though, stay away from Mrs. Holloman. This is still an ongoing investigation."

"All right, Detective, but I'm sure it will just turn out to be yet another of Alicia's paranoid delusions."

Alicia stretched the full length of bed when she awoke the next morning, feeling more refreshed than she had since no telling how long. Perhaps she benefited from indulging in only one glass of wine with her pizza the night before, despite how full that glass may have been. After Mason had gone, she had snuggled down into her warmest pajamas with pizza, wine, and *Casablanca*, and each time the memory of what had transpired between them encroached on her thoughts, she pushed it back down.

When she rolled her head up, she noticed the marks the handcuffs had left on the headboard. She drew her forefinger across them and smiled as a trill ran through her. The cuffs had left no lasting impression on her wrists, which left her oddly disappointed. Then she sat straight up in bed, flinging the covers off of her and covering her face with her hands. What the hell was the matter with her? The events of the night before had unfolded quite naturally, but now the morning light cast a shadow across every magical moment.

"Oh, God. What must he think of me?" she moaned into her hands. Then she lowered her arms and scowled. *What do I think of him?* she thought. He orders her around, cuffs her, puts his *thing* in her mouth—even spanks her!

She sucked in a sudden gasp of air with such force, she had to swallow to keep from coughing. "He must be into S&M!" *How typical for a cop to be a sadist!* So did he think she was a masochist? Except he hadn't caused her any pain, not really. In fact, she had never before experienced such pleasure. She leaned back against the headboard, closed her eyes, and basked in the memory. She had no idea what this meant for her now—for them! Were they boyfriend and girlfriend? They weren't exactly dating, but she couldn't wait for a replay of the night before.

With these thoughts and a mental note to call her attorney for a status on her pending divorce, Alicia went on to the master bath to shower, passing the tub and thinking about how he'd bathed her. He had saved her, bathed her, pampered her, pleasured her. She had given him complete control, and he had taken care of her. Never before had she felt so…cherished. And by a virtual stranger! What did this say about her? She resolved to embark on a thorough Internet search on the topic once she got out of the shower.

The steam from the shower rolled out when she opened the door, and she dried off and wrapped the towel around her chest before stepping out. She always preferred hot showers, so as usual the mirror had fogged over, but her blood ran cold at the sight of the words legible in the glass: YOU KNOW THE TRUTH

Alicia stared at the mirror until her breath returned, but her pulse continued to race in her chest. She peered around but found no evidence that anyone had come in during the few minutes she'd been in the shower. "Mr. Holloman?" she called out in a hoarse whisper. Then she remembered that, supposedly, she knew the man. "Danny?"

She wasn't too terribly surprised when no apparition appeared, although she had no clue how she would have reacted if one had. Could she be imagining it? A step closer brought it more clearly into focus: YOU KNOW THE TRUTH

Well, words written on a mirror had to qualify for a reason to call Mason, so she skipped into her bedroom and picked up her phone from the nightstand. His cell rolled straight to voicemail.

"Hi, Mason. It's Alicia…Pageant." *Oh, of course, just in case he's slept with another Alicia in the last forty-eight hours.* "You said to call if anything strange happened, well...jus-just call me back. Thanks."

As she walked back into the bathroom to snap a picture of the message with her phone, she dialed the other number Mason had programmed in, which rang at the homicide division. "Is Detective Crawley in, please?"

"No, he isn't in. Something I can help you with?" asked the man on the other end of the line.

But when Alicia looked back at the mirror, the fog had dissipated, and the words vanished with it. "N-no, thank you," she forced out before ending the call. Now she was relieved she hadn't reached Mason or he'd be calling the coroner to have her committed. The words *had* been there. Hadn't they? Or maybe she really was losing her mind.

She threw on jeans and a T-shirt then checked the alarm—still set—and the doors—still locked—before shrugging, turning off the alarm, and retrieving the morning paper. Padding barefoot toward the kitchen, she came to an abrupt halt as soon as it came into view.

Every drawer had been pulled out, every cabinet door thrown open.

That ice water ran through her veins yet again, and she rotated in a full circle. Nothing else appeared out of place. Why was he doing this to her? It had to be Daniel Holloman. None of this started until she witnessed whatever she had witnessed. She had never put much faith in the paranormal before, but recent events were converting her quickly. She pulled her cell from her pocket slowly, as if any sudden movement might disrupt...whatever. She redialed

Mason's cell. Voicemail.

"Hi, it's Alicia again. I-uh—" *I hate leaving Goddamn voicemails!* "Could you please call me back as soon as possible?" Then she called the station back. "Hi, has Detective Crawley come in?"

"No, ma'am, he's actually not scheduled to come in today. Is there something I could help you with?"

"No, thanks. He had told me to call him if I thought anything odd had happened. It's probably nothing. I think someone might have been in my kitchen."

"Someone's been in your kitchen?"

"Yes. At least I think so."

"Is anything missing?"

"Not that I can tell."

"Can I get your name?"

"Alicia Pageant. P-A-G-E-A-N-T."

"Do you want to report a robbery or breaking and entering? I can transfer you to that department."

"No, like I said, I'm not even sure, and Mason...Detective Crawley told me to speak to him directly."

The man on the other line said nothing for a moment. "What's your address? I'll send a squad car over just to check it out for you."

"No, that's all right. I'll just wait to hear back from him, but thanks."

"Well, until you do, don't touch anything. Leave it exactly as you found it until he gets there."

"Yes, I will. Thank you."

After they hung up, she glanced around the kitchen then stared longingly at the coffeemaker. *Damn it.* And she couldn't touch anything. She wondered if that restriction applied to the cold pizza in her refrigerator. She bit her bottom lip as she thought, then she spotted the peppermint next to the discarded pizza box on the kitchen counter. It must have come with her pizza order. *Surely one peppermint won't matter*, she decided as she grabbed the plastic-wrapped candy. Then she flopped down on the living room sofa with a huff...and shattered into a million pieces.

The tears had begun without preamble in a full and sudden onslaught of wracking sobs, the loss of control of her kitchen cabinets crushing her nascent optimism and scattering it to the wind. "Leave me alone!" she screamed through her tears, although still not certain to whom she cried out. At first she tried to hold back, but soon she surrendered to the full throes of panged, convulsive weeping.

She wanted a mulligan—a do-over of her life. As if all the regrets going back to grade school—save those recent few lost months—had come crashing into her consciousness, taunting her with each poor choice, every wrong path taken that had led her to this place—alone and afraid in a house with walls that both caged and concealed her, since she couldn't fathom facing whatever loomed beyond *this place of wrath and tears*. No, her head had been bloodied and bowed figuratively and literally through circumstance both of chance and of her own creation, leaving her to face the reality that her own poor judgment had rendered her powerless. She might have been the creator of her fate, but she was not its master, and the awareness descended over her like a black, wool blanket. She recalled a quote from Sophocles she'd learned in college, *The keenest sorrow is to recognize ourselves as the sole cause of all our adversities.*

Once she had gained a modicum of control, at least to the point she believed herself capable of coherent speech, she called Mason's phone again. Still voicemail, but this time his voice struck a chord with her, or strummed it rather, sending a vibration down her spine. She held her breath as she listened then pressed *End* and dialed again. He had never spoken harshly to her, even when he had riddled her with accusations. His dulcet intonations soothed her, rewinding her memory to the night before when he had stilled the perpetual motion of her thoughts and allowed her just to *be* there in that moment—not having to choose or to live with those choices. She had released herself to him, surrendered her power and reveled in the freedom.

As her weeping subsided, she submitted to the luxury of calling once again, closing her eyes and laying her head back. When he spoke, she felt safe. She squeezed the peppermint out of its plastic wrapper and popped it into her mouth as his message concluded. Then she ended the call and got up to go to her computer nook.

Chapter Five

Mason's eyes fluttered open, staring straight up at the old popcorn ceiling. He couldn't remember the last time he had woken up before his alarm—or feeling this well rested. The light reaching in through his window seemed brighter than usual, and the outside noises louder. *What time is it anyway?* He rolled over and reached for his watch on the nightstand then jumped out of bed. *Nine-fifty!*

"Fuuuuuuuuuuuuuuuuuuuuuuuuuuuuck!" He had been using his cell phone as an alarm clock for years, and, as always, he had plugged it in before going to bed, but now the son-of-a-bitch wouldn't even turn on! He stood staring at the black screen as if it would somehow provide an explanation when suddenly one dawned on him. He'd had it in his pocket when he jumped in the lake. "Goddamn it!" He threw the phone against the wall, but although being submerged in water for less than a minute had rendered it useless, it proved impervious to the force of the impact yet did manage to imprint a nice divot on the dingy wall.

Mason rushed through a shower then took off for the Apple Store where he borrowed a phone to call Alicia. Her line rang several times before rolling over to voicemail, but he figured she might not be answering an unfamiliar number.

"Alicia, it's Mason. Look, my cell phone died, so don't even bother trying to call me at that number right now. I'm in the process of getting a new one. I'll be heading over to the sheriff's station when I'm done here, but I'll give you a call as soon as I can." Although he would be making one additional stop on the way to the station, but he'd let that be a surprise for her later. The image of how he planned to use his intended purchases lightened his mood considerably.

Even given the circus-like atmosphere of the Apple Store on a Saturday, Mason acquired his new phone after far more time than he thought necessary, and he called Alicia again. Once again, it rang to voicemail. "It's Mason. I got a new phone. Same number. Give me a call if you need anything. Otherwise, I'll see you tonight." He stopped just short of saying he was looking forward to it. But he was—and his anticipation increased at the next shop as he selected certain accoutrements specifically for her.

"Didn't expect to see you here today," Captain Landry said as Mason walked around to his desk with a cup of burned coffee.

"I wanted to follow up on something—a missing person, I think."

"Buzz was looking for you."

Mason's face contorted as he swallowed the bitter sludge. "You know why?"

"Something about a B and E."

"Huh. I wonder what that's about."

As his captain walked off, Mason logged onto his computer and into the Unidentified and Missing People Repository and typed in *Heidi Doucet*.

Bingo. He knew he'd heard that name before. She'd been reported missing ten weeks before—just a couple of weeks after Alicia's accident. The profile outlined the basic information. Date of birth—only twenty-four. Red hair, blue eyes, height 67 inches, weight 130 pounds. A photograph of a cute girl who couldn't have been more different from Alicia in every aspect. He couldn't imagine Alicia having a confrontation with this ginger wisp.

The profile listed the Orleans Parish Sheriff's department as the agency handling the case, and he dialed the number of his contact in that office.

"Shelby."

"Hey, Shelby, it's Mason Crawley. How you doin'?"

"Not bad. What can I do for you?"

"I'm calling about a case you folks have down there, a girl who went missing."

"And you're thinking homicide?"

"I'm not thinking anything yet. It's Case number H 2698712."

"Got it. Hang on a minute." After a few moments, the detective returned to the line. "Yeah, I remember this one. Heidi Doucet—the cute redhead."

"Her last known address is up here," Mason said. "How did the case wind up in your jurisdiction?"

"Her car was found here, at the Port of New Orleans parking garage. She was supposed to be going on a cruise with her boyfriend, but she never made it onto the ship. No one even knew she had gone missing until after the cruise ship had returned and her parents hadn't heard from her."

Mason leaned forward in his chair and jotted down the information. "What did you find in the car?"

"Trunk full of suitcases, packed and ready to go. But get this—the interior of the car was completely wiped down, not a print anywhere."

Mason's brows drew together as he wrote *no prints* on his pad. "What about the boyfriend?"

"Never could find him."

"So he didn't make it onto the ship either?"

"No one else was ever registered to be in the cabin with her. She had told everyone she was going away with this guy—only name we got was 'John'—but no ticket was issued for him. No one had ever even met him—not her parents, not even her roommate."

"Did you check who paid for her cruise ticket?"

"She put it on her own credit card."

"What about her phone records?"

"Yeah, we dumped her phone. Plenty of calls back and forth with a disposable cell."

He tossed the pen on his desk. "And you're certain she went missing from the parking garage?"

"Well, we interviewed her roommate. Last time she saw Heidi was the day before the cruise. Supposedly, she and her boyfriend were going to spend the night down here and get on the ship in the morning."

"And what day was that?"

"Eighth of August."

The bile rose in Mason's throat, or perhaps it was

just that god-awful coffee coming back up. That was the day before Alicia's accident. "Could you give me the contact info on the roommate?"

Shelby recited the name, address, and contact number, then said, "What are you thinking, Crawley? Do you have a lead?"

"I might have an idea on the boyfriend, but let me follow up. I'll let you know."

After they hung up, Mason immediately called Karen Littlejohn. She answered on the first ring, probably after seeing Sheriff's Office on the caller ID. "Hello?"

"This is Detective Mason Crawley. I'm calling about your friend Heidi Doucet."

"Did you find her? Is she OK?"

"No, ma'am. We're pursuing some new information. Do you have time to meet with me this afternoon?"

"Um, sure. I can be home in about half an hour."

"Is this the home you shared with Miss Doucet?"

"Yes, sir."

"Good. I'll see you then."

Mason met up with her at the apartment complex within walking distance from campus. The apartment itself could have belonged to any student, with walls adorned with framed movie posters, old album covers, and two hybrid bicycles hanging from wall mounts, and the faint familiar stench of stale beer and weed.

The young, blond coed demonstrated none of the jitters typical for someone her age when speaking to a detective, the questioning most likely having become routine over the last two months. She repeated much of the same information Mason had gathered from Detective Shelby.

"And you have no idea who this 'John' person is?"

"No, sir." Though she still retained her calm demeanor, her downward gaze and the rising color in her cheeks told a different story.

"Miss Littlejohn, if you know something else, you need to tell me."

From the second-hand green couch where she sat with her hands twisted together, she turned her light brown eyes up to where he stood as they began to gloss over with tears.

"She said they were keeping their relationship on the down-low because he's faculty, and...he's married."

Mason didn't bother to write it down; he'd known this much already. "Why didn't you mention this to the other detectives?" Right then his cell phone rang. It was Buzz. He pressed *Decline*.

"I...I really thought she'd be back by now. I thought they'd just gone somewhere else, that his wife had found out about the cruise or something. Heidi said his wife went ballistic when he asked for a divorce."

This was quite a different story from the version Meador had given of having ended the affair. "That's no excuse for lying to the police. Do you realize how much time you wasted when we could have been pursuing this in our investigation?"

The tears streamed down her face, and she rubbed her sleeve across her nose. "I was just trying to protect her privacy. I didn't want her parents to know she was dating a married man, but there's no way she would go this long without calling me or them."

He shook his head and released a heavy sigh. College kids were idiots. "What else do you know about him? What department was he in?"

"Nothing. He said if anyone found out, he could get fired."

"*He* told you this?"

"No, Heidi."

"So you never spoke to him, never met him?" She shook her head. "You're still going to have to make a complete statement, and this time don't leave anything out. Try to remember everything you can, even the smallest detail. Has anyone else moved into her room?"

"No, her parents have been paying her rent." Karen stood and walked past him to open the door just past the bathroom.

"The last day you saw her," he asked as he flipped through the envelopes on Heidi's dresser, "what time did she leave?"

"Maybe four-ish. I didn't look at the clock. She said she was going to meet *him*, and they were leaving on the cruise in the morning."

"And she didn't come back?"

She shrugged. "Not that I know of."

"Did anyone come by here looking for her?"

"I don't think so."

"A petite brunette?"

"Not while I was here, but I went out that night. I really wouldn't know."

A search of Heidi's room turned up nothing, and Mason drove away from the complex with no more information than he'd had when he'd arrived—*except* someone had lied. Meador had told him, as well as Alicia, that he'd ended the affair, but he had told Heidi he was leaving his wife. Or maybe Heidi had just lied to her roommate, but that impressed Mason as the least likely scenario.

His cell rang again, and he answered. "Hey, Buzz. What's up?"

"Don't you ever answer your phone?"

"I was interviewing a witness?"

"All day? I left you two voicemails."

"Long story. I had to get a new phone. I didn't get the notifications. What's going on?"

"Alicia Meador called the station looking for you."

Mason winced at the words. *Aw, fuck!*

Buzz continued. "She sounded kinda upset. She said something about someone breaking into her kitchen?"

"Did you send a unit over?"

"She said she only wanted 'Mason'—and she used your first name. Something going on between you two?"

"I'll call her now."

"All right, Romeo, but I'd stay away from *that* one. I don't think she's exactly your type."

Mason smiled as he ended the call. *Ah, Buzz, how wrong you are!*

As written in the Murphy's Lawbook of traffic lights, Mason managed to hit an unprecedented number of green lights in succession when he most wanted an opportunity to stop. Once he rolled toward a yellow light as it turned red, he glanced at his phone. Sure enough, four voicemails.

"Hi, Mason. It's Alicia...Pageant. You said to call if anything strange happened, well...jus-just call me back. Thanks."

"Hi, it's Alicia again. I—uh—Could you please call me back as soon as possible?"

He skipped listening to Buzz's messages and instead immediately called Alicia. After five rings, it went to voicemail, and he realized he'd been getting her voicemail all day. *Shit.*

"Alicia, it's Mason. Call me back as soon as you get this message."

He had been headed back over to question Meador again, but that would have to wait. He pulled into a Winn Dixie parking lot to turn around and drove toward Lilac Lane. He had no idea what to expect when he got there. The tone of her messages rang more of discomfort than fear, or, damn it, even a wistful desire to see him. Buzz had mentioned her kitchen. Maybe her spoons had run off again.

On the other hand, what if Buzz recognized something Mason didn't want to admit? Last night had been relatively tame but intense nonetheless. Discovering the submissive within could be an emotional journey for Alicia, wrought with self-doubt and confusion. Although when he left she had given every indication of being well-pleased and satisfied, if hungry, morning might have brought with it embarrassment and regret.

The possibility unsettled but did not dissuade him. Yes, they'd only known each other a few days, but the night before had confirmed what he had suspected since their first kiss. They were a perfect fit. He wanted to protect her, take care of her, keep her safe. Alicia might need some convincing, but she needed this too. Once he solved the mysteries of Holloman and Heidi Doucet, he believed they had a future together.

Mason tried her number again. She still wouldn't take his call. He banged the heels of his hands against the steering wheel. Though he hadn't planned it, Mason knew he'd made a mistake to rush her like that. He resolved to take a step back, proceed at a slow pace that would allow her time to adjust and to tell him how she felt. They should have discussed it before doing anything—open, honest communication. But after she'd almost killed herself with that stunt in the lake, he had been compelled to take drastic action.

"Oh, fuck!" What if she'd taken another dive in the lake or done something else equally stupid. He pressed his foot harder against the accelerator.

Mason drove up to the house just as the sun slid beneath the horizon, but no light shone through any of the windows. He hesitated before grabbing the bag with his *special* purchases but decided, assuming the worst things waiting for him on the other side of that door were her fear and insecurities, they could at least use the items as props for discussion.

Before he had a chance to knock, the door opened, and Alicia flew into him, circling her arms around his neck, and covering his mouth with hers in a deep, hot, furious kiss. He stepped forward, dropped the bag, and knocked the door closed behind him with his foot while driving his tongue into her mouth and his fingers into her damp hair. In his wildest dreams, he wouldn't have imagined such a reception. Well, perhaps in his *wildest* dreams. Her breasts—braless under a thin T-shirt—pressed against his chest as the heat radiating from her body telegraphed a message straight to his groin, and he pressed his hips against hers.

God, she was hot—and no wonder. All the lights were out, but candles set upon every surface lit up the room, and she had a fire burning as well. He used both hands on either side of her head to break the suction she had on his mouth. Sweat beaded across her flushed face as she gasped for air, but his heart and breath raced as well.

"Alicia, why aren't you answering your phone?"

With eyes half closed and a tight jaw, she said, "I know what you are. You're a *dementor*."

He smiled and couldn't suppress a soft laugh despite her obvious disobedience. "A dementor. Like in Harry Potter? How much have you had to drink?" With his arm around her waist, he guided her to the couch and sat her down.

"No, I'm not drunk. I've been reading. I understand. You want me to be your sub. You want to dement me."

Comprehension hit him and knocked him down to the sofa beside her, and she laid her head against his shoulder. "You mean dominate," he said low, not quite sure if to her or to himself. So much for taking it slow.

"Yes! You're a dominator."

"You mean dominant." He turned and held her up to face him. "Alicia, how much have you been drinking?" In good conscience, he couldn't—or *shouldn't*—continue with her in this intoxicated state.

She leaned forward and pressed her lips to his. "Why do you keep asking me that? I know what I want. I want to be your submissive."

Closing his eyes, he dropped his forehead against hers. "Have you been a sub before?"

"Uh-uh."

"Then how do you know? What do you even know about it?" This poor little rich girl—the cotillion princess, coddled and abandoned in turn. Yes, *he* knew she needed this, but she had to be sure.

"I liked what we did last night, and I know what I read online. You can tell me the rest. Right? Isn't that how it works? Just tell me what to do."

Here he had thought she would be the one confused, and he had a cavalcade of emotions coursing through him—not the least of which being pure, unadulterated desire. He squeezed her neck and shoulders between his thumbs and fingers as he inhaled her hot breath. "You're sure this is what you want?"

"I feel safe when I'm with you, and…" She twisted into the massage with a throaty groan and rested her head against his chest.

"And what?"

"*I am melting and palpitating. I want to do things so wild with you that I don't know how to say them.*"

Good God. He gulped and wondered if she could feel his heartbeat throbbing against her cheek.

"Anaïs Nin," she said.

"What?"

"Anaïs Nin wrote that to Henry Miller."

He grasped her hair in his fist and pulled her head back. She gasped, as he had predicted, and he thrust his tongue deep into her mouth. If she was lucid enough to quote dead writers, then who was he to argue? His cock twitched in agreement with his decision—any more discussion could wait until morning.

Mason released her mouth and hair then took her hand and tugged her up and over to stand with him before the fire. With his lips on her ear, his whispered, "Take off your jeans and T-shirt, and get on your knees."

When he walked away, Mason glanced back just as she pulled her shirt over her head, baring her back to him, and he grinned. He retrieved the bag from where he'd tossed it by the front door and pulled out the pink leather wrist cuffs, about two inches wide, and a matching blindfold. He returned to find Alicia kneeling on the rug in front of the fire with her hands on her thighs and her face cast down, naked except for the blue silk covering her ass and *Australia*, her hard nipples a shade darker than the mocha sofa. The sight of her in this submissive pose with the golden firelight dancing across her luxuriant flesh, combined with the friction of his erection against his jeans, strengthened his arousal, and he couldn't wait to watch his cock disappear into her mouth.

"Very good, my pet," he said when he stood before her. He dropped the cuffs and blindfold on the coffee table beside her then he offered her his hand. "Come here. Stand up."

She took his hand and did as she was told, standing there as the flickering candlelight sparkled on her skin like sequins. "What should I call you?"

"You may call me 'Sir.' Now, give me your

wrists."

Alicia held out her arms, and he buckled a fur-lined pink cuff to each of her wrists, her breathing accelerating as he did so. He then picked up the blindfold and held it out for her to see. "I am going to cover your eyes now," he said and waited a moment for a reaction. She stared at the blindfold and bit her bottom lip but said nothing. "You can stop anything at any time with one word."

She nodded. "Yes." Then she added, "Sir."

He smiled and placed the blindfold over her eyes, adjusting it into position. He swept his hands over her breasts and pulled on both nipples at once, eliciting a delicious moan from Alicia. "You have such beautiful breasts, my pet." He twisted her nipples slightly, and she almost fell backward. He threw one arm around to support her before bending over to pull one of the beaded peaks into his mouth. He sucked hard, adding sibilance to her cries; yet despite the twinge of pain he knew it must cause, she didn't stop him but, instead, laid her hands upon his back as if to draw him closer.

He released her nipple with a resounding smack. Her back was hot and damp with sweat. He needed to get her away from the fire, but first he would render her further under his control. Settling her straight on her feet, he stepped back a few feet, and she sensed his absence.

"Where—" Her words floated out on puffs of breath. "Where are you going?"

"Shhhh. No questions."

When he touched her from behind, she started in surprise. His hand traveled down to caress the blue silk, and he ran his finger around beneath the lace waistband before deciding to have her keep it on. For now. Taking one of her wrists, he hooked a chain to the metal loop on the cuff then, pulling both hands behind her back, joined it to the loop of the other cuff so her wrists were chained together. Her chest rose and fell rapidly as he steered her to the bedroom— from apprehension or anticipation or perhaps a combination.

The thick carpet in the bedroom made it a better choice anyway. They stopped, and he walked in front of her just in time to see her lick those perfect pink lips. He took hold of the back of her head and kissed her, leaning into her just as she stretched up to meet him to deepen the kiss, urging him on with eager, hot passion. He had never known such fevered kisses before.

"Are you doing all right, my pet?" he asked once he finally forced himself to tear his mouth away.

"Yes, Sir."

"Good girl. Now, back on your knees." He helped her down then walked over to switch on the bedside lamp before turning around to admire her beautiful submission. She remained completely still, aside from the quick rise and fall of her chest, as he kicked off his shoes and undressed, his rock-hard cock directed at her like a dowsing rod pointing to water.

When Mason returned to her with silent steps and touched the side of her head, she reflexively turned her face upward even though she couldn't see. "You look amazing, my pet."

"I do?"

"God, yes. You are already a beautiful woman. To

have you bound and blindfolded on your knees like this, giving yourself to me with complete trust...you are breathtaking." He ran his fingers along her jaw and brought his thumb to her mouth, rubbing her bottom lip. She took his thumb into her mouth, the velvety warmth of her tongue escalating the urgency of his need.

Mason hooked his thumb on her bottom teeth to open her mouth and with his other hand brought the head of his cock to her lips. A guttural sound of recognition joined her heaving breaths, and the tip of her tongue licked the moisture that had developed on the crown. All of his blood rushed to his groin, leaving him lightheaded, as he watch her circle her tongue around the head of his cock then cover it with her lips with gentle suction.

When he unleashed a primal groan, she stopped. "Am I doing something wrong?"

He laughed and raked his fingers into the wet hair on the back of her head. "Oh, no. Not at all, my pet. Your lips are perfection." Then he guided her mouth accordingly and said, "Suck my cock."

Mason thought he saw the hint of a smile on her lips just before they consumed him, but after that, all thoughts were gone as he stood hypnotized—transfixed by the view, as if from a high altitude, of this woman in complete supplication, swallowing his cock into her sweet, hot mouth. He gripped her hair tighter to set the rhythm as her moans sent a heated vibration down his shaft.

God, she was hot. Too hot. *She's burning up!* How had he not noticed that his fingers clung to drenching wet hair? He used both hands on either side of her head to fight both the suction she had created with her clenched jaw and his own visceral instinct to push forward. Sweat dripped freely over his fingers as she gasped for air.

"Alicia, dear God, are you sick? You're burning up! Have you called a doctor? You have a terrible fever."

With her face tilted up to him, she spoke through her teeth. "I have a fever for you. For you, Mason. I am melting and palpitating for you."

He yanked off the soaking blindfold and she shut her eyes to the sudden light. Grabbing her arm none too gently, he lugged her toward the lamp and opened one of her eyes wide between his thumb and forefinger. The dilated pupil concealed all of the chocolate brown. What had she done now?

Mason sat on the bed with his head in his hands as Alicia panted on her knees mere inches from his rapidly-deflating penis. Idiot didn't begin to describe him. He couldn't have noticed her dilated pupils in the dim, candlelit living room, but the blistering heat emanating from her along with her uncharacteristic behavior—*Aw, shit!* He should have known she wouldn't just offer herself to him like this.

He hurriedly pulled on his jeans then unbuckled the cuffs from Alicia's wrist and helped her up. With his hands on her shoulders, he held her at arm's length and tried to force her to meet his eyes. "Alicia, what did you take?" he asked in a calm but firm voice.

With her teeth grinding and her eyes nearly rolling back into her head, she warbled out, "Nothing."

Mason shook her, and her head flopped around on

her neck. "What did you take!" he screamed.

"Nothing! I swear. I didn't take anything." She collapsed against his chest and nuzzled his neck. "Come on, Mason. I want you to take me and..." she whispered, "*fuck* me."

Yes, now he knew without a doubt she had taken something. "Goddamn it, Alicia! Where are your pills? How many did you take?"

She scrunched her face and whined. "Masooooon, stop yelling at me. They're by the kitchen sink, but I haven't taken any today."

He pulled her into the living room and tossed her roughly onto the suede couch where she immediately began nuzzling and stroking one of the cushions. Mason shook his head and, flipping on lights and blowing out candles in his path, marched to the kitchen. He stopped short, though, because every cabinet door, every drawer was wide open. What the hell had she been looking for? Drugs, perhaps?

Her meds were right where she had said they would be, and glancing at the date on the label and the number of pills, she hadn't taken more than prescribed—not too surprising considering her present condition. Her behavior was more indicative of illegal drugs—X maybe—than an overdose. He poured a glass of water then returned to the living room and sat on the coffee table in front of where she lay smiling and petting the sofa.

"Sit up!" She didn't move at first, so he pulled her upright and held the glass to her lips. "Drink, Alicia. You're going to get dehydrated." She gulped the water down greedily, and he set the empty glass down then gripped her upper arms to force her attention.

"Now, I'm going to ask you one more time. What did you take?"

She stared at him through giant black eyes. "Nothing."

"*What did you take!*"

"You said you would only ask once more."

He dropped his chin to his chest and blew out a frustrated exhalation.

"And you keep yelling at me," she whined. "That's one of the things I liked about you—you didn't yell. I don't want to be your sub if you yell at me."

"Then we'll put in our agreement that I will only yell at you when you take drugs," he said. "Now, if you do not answer me, Alicia, I will have to punish you."

She leaned forward and spoke low in his ear. "Promise?"

"I mean it. I will bend you over my knee right now and spank you if you don't tell me what you are on."

She ran her tongue around his ear and nibbled the lobe, and damn it if he didn't feel a twinge of arousal returning. "Then let's get started," she said.

"That's it, Alicia. I'm not screwing around. Either tell me what you took or I'm going to—"

Before he could finish, Alicia was on his lap kissing him. When she wrapped her arms around his neck, he tried to pull her off, but it was as if whatever she'd taken had given her superhuman strength. He wrestled with her until he had her flat on her back on the sofa, and he pushed himself up and held her down with his hands on her arms and his calf across her thighs. He stared down at this near-naked woman enflamed with lust, lips swollen and chafed, the drugs rendering her combustible. Ignoring his own growing desire, he sat down and maneuvered her around and across his lap as her laughter echoed off the high ceilings.

Mason brushed his hand over her blue silk-covered ass and allowed himself a moment's indulgence in sliding down the crevice to between her legs, making her wiggle and squeal. "Since you will not obey me, you must be punished." With that, he raised his hand high and slapped it down hard on her right cheek.

"Ack! Mason!"

As he rubbed away the sting, he asked, "Do you have something to say, my pet?"

"Do the other side."

Thwack! "Now?"

But she just giggled and squirmed, grazing her tummy against his reviving erection. As she dampened beneath his fingertips, he realized this was getting them nowhere—or at least in the wrong direction. They were both getting turned on and he was getting pissed off, and a Dom must never discipline in anger. He'd have to try a different tactic.

"All right, my pet. No more spankings until you tell me what you took."

Even with her mouth against the couch cushion, he could still make out her words. "I didn't take anything."

"Alicia, you are obviously on drugs, and I—"

"Oh, my God," she said, raising her head. "I'm on drugs."

"What did you take?"

She pushed herself off his lap and crossed her arms across her chest. "I didn't take anything."

"You *are* on drugs!"

"I'm on drugs!"

"What did you take?"

"What did I take?"

"Stop doing that!" Mason jumped off the couch and combed his fingers through his hair.

"Stop doing what?"

"Repeating everything I say."

"I'm not." She slid off the sofa and crawled to where she had discarded her T-shirt and pulled it over her head.

"You admit you are on drugs."

"Yes, but I didn't take them."

"Oh, they just *flew* into your mouth," he said, flinging his arm in an exaggerated gesture, "or up your nose or in your vein."

She shook her head and covered her flushed cheeks with her hands. She needed more water. Mason jerked the glass off the table and stomped back into the kitchen.

"Oh, and what the hell have you done in here?" he called out, slamming a few cabinets and drawers shut.

"It wasn't me. It was Mr. Holloman…haunting me."

"Naturally."

"Th-that's why I w-was calling you this m-morning." She sat shivering by the fire when he returned with her water, even as the perspiration soaked through her shirt. "I w-woke up, and th-they were like that."

Then, like a 3-D image suddenly coming into focus, all of the pieces fell into place for Mason as another wave of the drug's effects rolled over her. He just had time to crouch beside her before she would no longer have been able to sit up on her own.

"Alicia, I'm so sorry. I should have known." She stopped grinding her teeth long enough to drink some of the water he offered, then he carried her into the bedroom. He pulled off her wet shirt and laid her back against the pillows, but she captured his neck in the circle of her arms and drew him closer to her with a smile.

"Aren't you going to join me? I want to feel you inside of me."

He wiped the wet hair from her forehead. "That's just the drugs talking."

"N-no, it's not. H-how can you think that after last night? I want you now, Sir."

Her struggle to prevent her eyes from rolling back made that difficult to believe. "I want to get you to the ER. You have no idea what these kinds of drugs can make you say or do."

"Yes, I do. Th-that's why I think I'm on drugs and not just losing my mind. It's just lowering my…" She furrowed her brow. "What are those things that keep you from doing what you want to do?"

"Inhibitions?"

"That's it. They lowered my inhibitions, but this is what I want."

"I want to take you to the hospital."

"It'll still be there," she said as she pulled him down, his bare chest against her breasts, then removed whatever arguments might have remaining on the tip of his tongue with her fervent kiss.

Yes, the hospital wasn't going anywhere. His cock sprang to life, sending Mason a clear signal that this better not be another false alarm. As he sank deeper into her, deeper into the kiss, he squeezed her right breast and teased her nipple into a hard peak. Then he trailed his hand down and slid his fingers beneath that blue silk, over her wet clit, and into her hot core—hotter still from her fever. When he pushed and swirled two fingers inside of her, she loosened her hold on him and let her head fall back with a sultry moan.

Mason rolled the blue silk with slow deliberation down her legs as she writhed and purred, then he had his jeans off in two seconds flat and climbed on the bed and between her thighs. He fought the urge to dive right in when the drug so clearly held her in its throes. Taking her in this condition could be tantamount to rape—a battle of wills between cock and conscience. He leaned forward and held her head so she would face him.

"Alicia," he said softly. "Alicia, look at me." Her heavy eyelids lifted enough for him to see her black eyes, and a bright smile cut across her face. "Say something, my pet."

"Now, Sir."

And with that, he plunged into her in one swift move. She ran her fingers into his hair and brought his head back down, moaning into his mouth as she raised her hips up to meet him and match his tempo. A force stronger than gravity pulled him deeper still, and he grasped her hips, lifting them higher to drive his cock into her heat with full purchase. Alicia accompanied each thrust with a growling gasp. He had no idea if it was from pleasure or pain, but he could no sooner have stopped at this moment than he could have launched himself to the moon. Then her tight sheath constricted around his cock, and he thought she must be close to coming. He lowered her hips but pushed her knees back and rolled his finger around her clit until she cried out and convulsed around him, which was all it took for his own orgasm to burst forth, and he erupted inside of her.

He collapsed beside her and covered her face with kisses. "How do you feel?"

"Hmmm…like Lucy."

"Lucy?"

"Yes, the Beatles' *Lucy in the Sky with Diamonds*. I see kaleidoscopes in my eyes."

.

Chapter Six

The ER had enough gunshots, accidents, car crashes, and people who had simply waited until Saturday night before deciding they were sick enough to need medical treatment, to keep them occupied for days if not weeks.

After a period of recovery from what had to be the most incredible and explosive sexual experience of his life, Mason still insisted on taking Alicia to the ER, but she refused to go anywhere without taking a cool shower first. He agreed as long as he showered with her since she still was periodically overcome with waves of the effects of the drug, making balance a challenge even when not standing on a slick surface. Besides that, they both smelled strongly of sex. But once in the shower together, despite the temperature of the water, after he soaped up her breasts and pulled her nipples into stiff points and she demonstrated her proficiency on her knees with her wrists unbound, he pushed her up against the shower wall and wrapped her legs around his waist as he slipped into her with ease. He pumped into her with the same rhythm he used with his tongue in her mouth and came again when he had thought he had nothing left to give.

The ER waiting room overflowed with patients and their friends and/or family, and one group had even turned the occasion into an excuse for a picnic. Mason used his credentials to get Alicia triaged and in an exam room with the understanding that they were still looking at quite a wait. Something about the sterility of the hospital, exposed fully-dressed under the harsh fluorescent lights, had transformed Mason back into his detective persona as he stood next to where she sat with her feet dangling off the side of the hospital bed.

"I'm going to bring all your pills to the crime lab," he said, "since someone—whoever came into the kitchen—must have tampered with them."

"No," she said, rubbing her sore jaws. "I never took any of my meds today. Except for the water you gave me, I haven't had anything to eat or drink all day."

"Are you sure? What about coffee this morning?"

She yawned and shook her head. "When I couldn't reach your cell, I called the sheriff's station. They told me not to touch anything."

"When was the last thing you had anything to eat or drink?"

"Just the pizza last night, and…"

"And what?"

"And wine." She blushed and grinned. "Are you going to *punish* me for breaking your rules?" She reached for his neck but he took hold of her wrists and brought them back down. "Or do the spankings last night count as 'time served'?"

He cringed. "So you remember that. Do you?"

"I remember everything—*Sir*." The smile lit up her face and even made its way into her eyes, which were beginning to reveal that chocolate he loved so much.

"Alicia, I cannot begin to tell you how sorry I am about tonight, with the cuffs and the blindfold."

"You didn't enjoy it?"

"That's beside the point. I had no idea you had been drugged. I never would have taken advantage of you if I had."

She dropped her head and went silent. Then she sniffed, and he lifted her face up with his thumb to see tears in her eyes. "Hey, hey!" he said in a tender tone, as if appeasing a child. "What's the matter?"

"You don't want me…as your submissive."

He wiped a tear away with his thumb then held his hand against her cheek. "Of course I do. It's just you were drugged—against your will. I wasn't sure if you even knew what you were saying. You can't go jumping into something like this without a clear head."

"I had a clear head when I decided. At least I think I did. But I want it, Mason. I want to try."

She leaned her head on his shoulder, and he wrapped his arm around her. "How do you know?"

She sighed. "I'm so tired. I just want you to take care of me."

"Well, I've done a piss-poor job of it so far. I should have come to check on you as soon as I couldn't reach you."

"I tried calling you."

"I know. I'm sorry. I had to get a new phone after our little dip in the lake, and then I was checking on something…about Heidi Doucet."

She went rigid beneath his arm. "Oh."

"Did you ever meet her?"

"No, I don't think so, but I don't remember much…" She squinted, staring off beyond the institutional walls into nothing. "Wait. I think I do remember seeing her. She had red hair, but this doesn't make any sense."

He rubbed his hand up and down her arm. "What doesn't make sense?"

"I must have dreamt it or something. I see her sleeping, and she's lying down in grass."

"Do you remember anything else?"

"I'm kneeling beside her, and she's asleep in the grass, but it must be at my house because she's by the lake. And it's night." His hand stopped moving. "Why are you checking up on my husband's mistress?"

"She's missing. No one's seen her for three months."

At the tap on the door, they separated, and a doctor in scrubs walked in looking over the pages on a clipboard. "So, Ms. Pageant, you think you were drugged?"

Mason stepped forward to offer him his hand, which the doctor shook without glancing up. "I'm Detective Crawley. This is part of an ongoing investigation. We need to get the results of the drug screening back as soon as possible."

"Let's see what we find out first. Shall we?" The

doctor listened to her heart. "Do you know what you may have taken or how it might have been administered to you?"

"No, I haven't had anything to eat or drink since last night except for a couple of glasses of water that Detective Crawley gave me."

"When did the effects begin?"

"I'm not really sure."

He shone a tiny light in her eyes. "Uh-huh. But you're certain you were drugged."

"I, uh, I think so. I did a little experimenting as a teenager."

"And it felt the same? What do you think? Ecstasy? LSD?"

"No, I don't think so. I guess it could have been, but it was different."

"Uh-huh." The doctor stood up, jotted something down on the chart, then peered at her. "And you've had nothing else to eat or drink—no one gave you anything, no drinks or candy?"

She blinked and looked up at him. "I had a peppermint this morning."

"A peppermint?" Mason and the doctor asked in unison.

"Yes," she said, glancing from one to the other. "I think it came with the pizza."

The doctor wrote something else down then said, "Someone will be in to take a blood sample shortly, and then you'll have an IV for dehydration, but you should be fine."

"Thank you, doctor," they said to him as he walked out, closing the door behind him.

"Why didn't you mention the peppermint before?"

Mason asked the moment they were alone.

She shrugged. "I didn't think of it until he said candy. It was in a sealed wrapper. Besides, why would the pizza delivery guy want to drug me?"

"You're sure the mint came with the pizza?"

She couldn't answer, so she changed the subject. "So, if I'm your pet, do I get a collar?"

Taken aback by the question, he barked out a startled laugh. "Do you *want* a collar?"

"I guess it depends."

He stroked her hair, and she leaned her head into his hand. "Depends on what?"

"On the collar. Do I get any say in the matter? I saw some really nice ones."

"I see…" He kissed her temple. "I suppose that's negotiable."

"I mean, I have no idea how much a detective's salary is."

With a grin, he squeezed her cheeks and gazed into her eyes. "I can already tell you're going to be a brat," he said before kissing her puckered lips.

Alicia and Mason returned to the house on Lilac Lane early Sunday morning exhausted, neither having slept for over twenty-four hours.

"I'm so tired," she said as she schlepped into the kitchen, pantomiming efforts to make coffee, "I don't even know if I can make it into the bedroom."

Mason walked up behind her and, wrapping his arms around her waist, kissed the back of her neck. "Shall I carry you to bed? I thought I would join you again, but this time we'd actually sleep."

She leaned back against him and lifted her face to meet his kiss. The voices from across the lake caught their attention at the same time, and together they walked over to the door leading to the terrace. Alicia inhaled sharply and thought she might faint when she opened the door.

"Who is that with Mrs. Holloman?" Mason asked.

"Daniel. Daniel Holloman." Somehow, even with all her lapses of memory, she recognized him on sight, there on the deck with Jude rearranging the furniture. "He's alive."

"That's good—one mystery solved."

"Then you and John were right all along. But who's been moving my spoons?"

"You didn't seriously think it was a ghost. Did you?" Mason ran his hand down her back and up again. "I'm going over there to talk to him. You'll be all right for a little while?"

She responded with a half-nod and continued to stare at her neighbors as his footsteps faded off and the front door opened and closed. Her cell phone started ringing from the sofa outside. *So that's where it's been all this time.* When she stepped out onto the terrace, the Hollomans spotted her and smiled and waved. She waved back and picked up her phone. It was John calling.

"Hello?"

"Hi, Alicia. I haven't talked to you in a few days. Just wanted to see how you were doing. So…how's everything been?"

She closed her eyes and rubbed her temple, lack of sleep and the morning sun fostering a headache. How could she possibly begin to describe all of the bizarre occurrences since she'd seen him a week before? And now, her strongest—and most ludicrous—hypothesis had been disproven.

"It's been kind of a strange week, but you'll be happy to know you were right about one thing. Daniel Holloman is alive and well."

"Oh?"

"Yes." At that moment, Mason arrived at the Holloman residence and joined the couple on the deck. "Detective Crawley is over there talking to them now."

John blew into the phone. "Good. I'm glad that's all over. You see—it was all in your imagination."

"Well, if that's the case, my imagination is far more vivid than I ever imagined."

"What do you mean?"

But she lacked the energy and the initiative to discuss the odd happenings in her kitchen and lingerie drawer with her ex-husband. Instead, she asked, "Did you know that Heidi Doucet is missing?"

Silence.

"John? Are you there?"

"I'm here."

"Did you hear what I said? Your little girlfriend is missing. No one has seen her in three months."

"Who told you that?"

"Mason. Detective Crawley. He's investigating her disappearance."

He said nothing for several moments. "You really don't remember."

"Remember what?"

"Are you alone?"

Alicia glanced across the lake to where Mason and the Hollomans remained engaged in serious conversation. She walked back into the house and pulled the door closed. "Yes, I'm alone."

"I'm on my way."

"Wait. Why do you have to come over? What can't you tell me over the phone?"

"We can discuss it when I get there. Just don't say anything to anyone, and make sure you're alone—especially make sure that detective isn't there."

"John, you can't just expect me to take orders from you without an explanation. You have to give me something."

"There was an accident, Alicia. Heidi's dead. I'll be there in twenty minutes."

Before the call had even ended, she had released the phone, and it dropped to the floor. That same familiar thunderbolt of blinding light, pain, and paralysis overwhelmed her, accompanied by a sudden onset of tinnitus and a chill, as if they had taken liters of her blood at the hospital instead of just a sample. She tried to cough, to dislodge whatever clogged her throat, choking her, and she thought she might be sick.

She heard her name being called from a distance but getting closer, louder, until the voice screamed in her ear. "Alicia!" Only then did she realize Mason was shaking her.

"What's wrong?" he asked, his red-rimmed blue eyes darkened with worry. "Do I need to take you back to the hospital?"

She raised a hand to her throbbing temple and shook her head. "No, I'm fine—just exhausted. You should go." She stepped away from him, but he followed.

"What are you talking about? I thought we had decided I was going to stay."

"I need to get some rest. I think it would be better if you go." She forced a smile. "You know if you stay, we probably won't get any sleep."

That seemed to placate him, and he returned her smile as he traced his finger down her cheek. "Don't you at least want to know about the mysterious disappearance of Daniel Holloman?"

"Oh, yes, of course! Where has he been all week?"

"On a business trip, as a special contractor for the Department of Defense. And, yes, he *was* shooting at a snake. He apologizes for disturbing your sleep. He just didn't want to leave his wife alone all week with a snake in the grass."

"I guess I look foolish. You and John tried to tell me it was just my overactive imagination. I suppose what I thought was her dragging a body into the trunk was just him packing for the trip."

"Uh, well, maybe. They weren't really sure what you might have seen."

"I must apologize, Detective. It appears I really did call you out on a wild goose chase."

He held her close against his body. "Don't you ever apologize for that. I'm going to have to send Randy Bozeman an eighteen-year-old bottle of Scotch for getting sick and letting me take his shift. I might have started out chasing a wild goose, but instead I caught a beautiful pet."

Heat rose in her cheeks, and she closed her eyes as she accepted his gentle kiss. She wondered at the time. She had to get him out of there before John arrived.

"Besides," he said with a quick tap on her nose, "you have given me plenty of other mysteries to solve, like your missing spoons and open drawers and how you were drugged."

"Oh."

He released her and headed toward the front of the house. "And—last but not least—the disappearance of Heidi Doucet." He opened the door. "I'll see you tonight." And with those parting words, he was gone.

What was it Mason had said? She couldn't seriously believe there was a ghost? She did. She was being haunted, all right—just not by the ghost she had thought.

She looked up and around the high ceilings. "Heidi?"

Alicia's hands trembled as she reached for the doorknob even though she knew who had rung the bell.

"Hi, Alicia." John bent over as if to kiss her, but she stepped back and out of his way. He didn't share her nerves; he walked in with a dead calm and the proprietary confidence of a man coming home. She closed and locked the door before turning around to find he had seated himself on the couch and waited for her. "Come sit down. We need to talk."

She didn't want to do as he said not just merely from recalcitrance. Even though they had lived in that house together for years, being in the dimly-lit room with him now set her on edge. She decided to open the blinds on the windows facing east to let in the morning sun.

As Alicia started to sit in the chair near the couch, John held his hand out to her. "Come sit next to me." When she took her place beside him, he didn't let go of her hand but instead rubbed it between both of this. "My sweet Alicia, I had hoped this day would never come. I have dreaded it."

"What day?"

"When I would have to tell you the truth."

"Tell me what happened. You said Heidi was killed in an accident. Was she in the car with me?"

"No, it wasn't a car accident."

"Everyone thinks she's missing. Why don't the police know?"

"Because I've been trying to protect you."

"Protect me? Protect me from what?"

"Don't you remember anything?"

"I…I'm not sure. It's hazy, and it doesn't make sense." She wrenched her hand from his grip and rubbed her pounding temple. "Just images, like from a dream. It's night, and she's asleep in the grass by the lake." Alicia closed her eyes to pull the memory into focus—the smell of the dank night air, the soggy ground seeping through to her knees. "I'm kneeling beside her, trying to wake her up, and I'm…" *Crying?*

"She wasn't sleeping, Alicia. She was dead. You killed her."

"What!" She jumped and turned with such force, she almost fell backward onto the coffee table. "No." She shook her head and didn't stop, even as the pain increased. "I don't believe you."

John stood and reached for her hand, but she walked away from him. "It was an accident," he said. "You pushed her, and she hit her head."

"Why? Why would I have pushed her?"

"You went to confront her. Even though I told you I had broken it off with her, you wouldn't let it go until you'd had it out with her. You'd been drinking, and you ran out of here before I could stop you."

"So I just went to her house and shoved her?" Then a splinter of light in the shroud of darkness. *No, no.* "Wait—I remember driving up to the house." She could see the girl with red hair pacing frenetically in front of the window.

"Yes, that's right. Then you called me, hysterical. You said the two of you had argued and at some point you shoved her, and she hit her head on the corner of the desk."

She scoured her brain for some recollection. "I…I don't remember."

"I'm sure that's better, my dear. It's probably too traumatic to remember. Maybe we shouldn't talk about it anymore."

"No, we have to. I…I think she's haunting me."

"Haunting you?" he asked with an arched brow. "How would she be haunting you?"

"She…she's been moving my things, turning on lights, and opening drawers, and she left me a message on my mirror. She…she says I know the truth. I just can't remember."

"Alicia, don't be ridiculous. There's no such thing as ghosts."

The pain throbbed in her head until she thought

her skull might burst and reminded her she hadn't slept in over twenty-six hours. She closed her eyes and massaged her scalp, twisting her hair with her fingertips. "Just tell me what happened next."

"When I got there, she was dead. You were devastated, horrified. You begged me to help you."

"What did you do?"

"We put the body into an old duffel bag, then I put it into the trunk of your car."

"Oh, God." As more images emerged, tears filled her eyes. "That night, when I thought Danny Holloman had been murdered. It had been a dream— a memory—of us disposing of Heidi's body!"

Laying his hand on her shoulder, he asked, "Have you heard enough?"

"No, go on. I have to know everything."

"We drove to a secluded area near the campus lakes and buried her. That's when you saw her 'sleeping' in the grass. We couldn't bury her in the duffel bag because it could be traced back to us. But then…"

"But then what?"

"You were so guilt-ridden, you said you couldn't live with yourself. Before I could stop you, you got in your car and drove into the lake."

She wept freely now and stared up at him. "Then my accident—I was trying to kill myself?" A flash of her willingness to succumb to drowning only two nights before.

He pulled her into his arms and held her head against his chest. "Yes, but thank God, you survived."

"But you weren't there the night of the accident," she said. "Maddie told me the police didn't find you until the next day."

"I would have called 911 if no one else had shown up, but how was I supposed to explain what I was doing there? Once I was sure the paramedics were on the way, I had to go back to get rid of Heidi's car."

"We have to tell the police."

His muscles tightened around her. "Alicia, we can't. You'll be charged with murder, and I'll be an accessory."

"But her parents have a right to know. And, besides, it was an accident."

"After all this time and all we did to cover it up, do you think they will believe it's an accident?"

She pushed back and peered up at him. "But an autopsy could show it was an accident!"

"Where we buried her, I know the composition of the soil. The body would be too decomposed for a thorough autopsy."

"But people who care about her are looking for her. You! You once cared about her!"

He kissed her forehead. "I care about you more."

"She's never going to stop haunting me until I tell the truth!"

"Now tell me how she's haunting you."

"She put all of my bras in the refrigerator. She moved all of the spoons. She turns on the lights and opens the drawers and cabinets. And she wrote in the steam on the bathroom mirror, 'you know the truth.'"

"Alicia, don't you see. A ghost isn't doing those things. You are. Just like with your accident, the guilt has been torturing you. You have been terrorizing yourself."

She pulled away from him and turned around,

wrapping her arms around herself. The clarity of truth chilled her to the bone—the anagnorisis of her own Greek tragedy. Blood rushed to her head and then out again, leaving her chilled and dizzy. How could she have been so blind to something so transparent? With all the doors locked and the alarm secure, no one else could have been in the house, so she had conjured an apparition from thin air as the most *logical* explanation.

Then she thought of something. "But I was drugged!"

"Drugged?"

"Yes. Just yesterday. I was…I was really rolling hard. Someone must have drugged me with X or something."

"Are you sure?"

"I'm almost positive."

"Then isn't it possible you might have found some X left over from your wilder days?"

If she had been the one going through all of her own drawers and cabinets, she supposed anything could be possible.

John walked around to face her. "Alicia, you need me. Please, let me take care of you. If I'm here with you, I can keep your demons at bay. I know I made a mistake, but I never stopped loving you. Give me another chance—give *us* another chance. Trust me. We can get through this together. I'll always protect you. And as long as we're married, no matter what happens, they can't make me testify against you."

Testify? "I…I don't know. I need some time to think. I need to get some rest."

He rubbed his hands up and down her arms. "You

look exhausted."

"I haven't slept since night before last."

"That's not good for you. You're still recovering from your head injury." He pushed her hair off her shoulder, an innocuous gesture that he'd probably made a hundred times over the years, but today he just kept touching her, and every time it make her skin crawl.

She stepped back and rubbed her eyes. "I just hope I can sleep after everything you've told me."

"I think I left some zolpidem here. Shall I get you one?" She nodded, and a few minutes later he returned with the pill and some water. After she swallowed it, he said, "You get some rest. I don't want to disturb you, so why don't you just call me when you wake up?" She nodded again. "Good. Now come lock up after me and set the alarm." He kissed her on the top of her head, and she followed him to the door, locking up behind him as he had instructed.

Chapter Seven

Even with her head sandwiched between two pillows, Alicia couldn't muffle the sound of the incessant banging. Just when it would stop long enough for her to fade off with the false sense that it had finally ended, it would start up again. *Who would be doing construction at this hour?* she thought groggily before realizing she had no idea of the hour. As the banging began again, she flopped back with an indignant growl, throwing a pillow off her face, only then realizing that the banging—interspersed with the doorbell ringing—was actually someone knocking on her front door.

"Some people can be so inconsiderate," she mumbled as she somehow managed to drag herself out of bed and into the open living area.

Before she made it halfway to the door, she stopped and began to scream. She didn't stop screaming, either, when the knocking changed to hard blows against the door followed by a splintering crash as Mason burst in, setting off the shrieking burglar alarm to add to the cacophony. He rushed to her side and folded her into his arms, holding her head against his chest facing away from the sight of her distress.

Every single wine glass had been taken down from the hanging rack and set on the kitchen island, filled with a perfect measure of Bordeaux.

Mason spoke to her soothingly, words like, "Shhh, baby," and, "Everything's going to be all right," and, "What's your alarm code?" Once her screams had been reduced to sobs, she managed to croak out the four-digit number. He let her go sooner than she would have wanted, but at least when he punched in the code, it brought an end to that terrible screeching. Still, within a minute her cell rang. He found her phone where she'd left it on the floor and answered it.

"Yes, this is Detective Mason Crawley with the sheriff's office. I am on the premises now." Then to Alicia, he asked, "What's your alarm passcode?"

"A-apple," she stuttered out.

"Really?" he asked with his brows raised.

She nodded. "I changed it."

"Apple," he repeated to the responder.

If he said anything else to the person on the phone, Alicia didn't hear, too rapt in the vision of crimson in crystal. She jumped when he placed his hands on her arms from behind.

"That's it," he said. "I'm not leaving you again. I would have you stay with me, but I don't think you'd appreciate the amenities of my one bedroom apartment. The first thing I'm going to do is have this place dusted for fingerprints." He pulled out his phone, but she grabbed his wrist.

"No! No, it's not necessary."

"Alicia, someone is screwing with you. Someone has been breaking into your house, messing with your stuff, *drugging* you. We have to proceed on the assumption that you are in danger. Whoever it is could escalate and cause you serious bodily harm."

Turning away from him, she covered her eyes with her hands, hoping to stave off the tears, and shook her head. "You saw for yourself it's not possible. The doors were locked, the alarm was set. No one broke in here."

Although he did not raise his voice, his tone conveyed his aggravation nevertheless. "Don't tell me you're still entertaining your ghost theory. Holloman isn't even dead!"

"No, I know that."

"Then what is it? Talk to me."

Talk to him. God, what could she say? She needed more time, time to think. She desperately wanted to trust him—she had meant every word she'd said the night before. Until this moment, he had made her feel safe, protected. But what if she told him the truth—confessed everything? He was still a cop, and he'd only known her a few days. He'd have no choice but to arrest her. Would he believe it was an accident? Would he believe she couldn't remember what happened?

A lawyer—that's what she needed. She would call her attorney first thing in the morning. In the meantime, she had to get Mason out of there. No matter what happened, she knew they had no future together. If she didn't tell him the truth, they would always have this lie between them. If she confessed, he'd know she had killed a girl and done everything in her power to conceal the crime.

She wiped away the tears before she faced him. "I did it."

"You did what?"

"I put the wine in the glasses. I moved the spoons and my bras. I did it all."

He blinked back his confusion. "Why would you do that?"

"I've been doing it in my sleep. You were right to begin with—a combination of my pills and wine and the head injury. Don't you see? It's the only explanation."

He peered at her through narrowed eyes then glanced up at the empty rack. "You can't even reach most of those glasses. Are you saying you got a stool or something to stand on to get them all down?"

She shrugged. "I must have."

"And then you opened a bunch of bottles and did all this."

She walked over to where the empty bottles were lined up along the kitchen counter like the infantry and waved her hand before them. "Even the wine I poured—only my favorite. Who else would know which wines to select?" Except one bottle struck her as odd, and she picked it up, studying the label. *2010 Château Lafite Rothschild.* "This is weird," she said more to herself than him.

Mason strode to her side and took the empty bottle. "What's weird about this one?"

"That's a $1200 bottle of wine."

"You can afford it. Can't you?"

"Yes, but it's not even drinkable until 2025."

"You bought a $1200 bottle of wine that you can't even drink?"

"Well, I can't now. It's ruined. That was a stupid thing for me to do, even in my sleep."

He set the bottle aside and grasped her shoulders, staring at her with those stormy blue eyes. "You've been doing all this crazy shit in your sleep, and you're worried about the vintage? Come on. I want you to come with me to my place to pack up some things. If I'm here with you, I'll make sure you stay in bed—even if I have to tie you to it." He punctuated this last bit with a smile, but when he tried to pull her along, she resisted.

"No, Mason. I don't think that's a good idea."

"Which part? Coming with me to the apartment or me keeping you in bed?"

Pulling herself free from his hold, she walked over to the wall of windows and stared out at the lake. "Either. Both. Now that we know Mr. Holloman is all right, there's really no reason to see each other anymore."

"What the hell are you talking about?" When she didn't reply, he marched up behind her and jerked her around. "What about the last two nights? Yesterday you were picking out collars. What about all your talk about wanting to be my submissive, needing me to take care of you?"

"It's just like you said. It was the drugs. I didn't mean it."

"Like hell you didn't." He took hold of her upper arms and held tight when she tried to pull away. "And about those drugs—if you've been doing all this in your sleep, where did the drugs come from?"

"I probably had some leftover ecstasy or molly or something." Her eyes brimmed with tears, but there was nothing she could do to stop them.

"And you just took it and didn't remember." He burrowed his fingers into her arms. "What aren't you telling me, Alicia?"

"Nothing. Please, you're hurting me. Please go."

"You have to trust me."

"I do trust you." But she couldn't meet his eyes.

"In your research, did you read the three tenets of a Dom/sub relationship?"

She closed her eyes and nodded. "*Safe, sane, and consensual.*"

"No, that's any BDSM. Dominance and submission is about *trust, honesty, and communication.*" His words brought on more tears, and he pulled her into his arms close to his heart. "Trust me, Alicia."

She squeezed her eyes tight and sobbed. "I do, but I can't be your sub."

"If you trust me, then prove it." Releasing her from his embrace, he took her hand and dragged her into the bedroom.

"Please, Mason, why won't you believe me?"

"Because I know you were telling the truth all those other times when I doubted you, so now I *know* you're hiding something." In her bedroom, he retrieved the bag he had left there with the cuffs and blindfold then spoke softly in her ear. "Take off your clothes."

"No, I told you. I don't want to be your sub."

"I don't believe you. I think you want this from me. You need this. But something has happened, and you are hiding it from me."

"No, I swear it." The lie crept up from deep within her and heated her face.

"Do you trust me?"

"Yes."

He pulled out four lengths of black silk rope, each about five feet long. "Do you trust me enough to let me put these on you? To leave yourself open and helpless to me?"

"Please, Mason, I am not in the mood for sex games."

"I didn't say anything about sex. Or games. Do you trust me enough to let me put these on you?"

Scores of thoughts buzzed through her mind as she stared at the ropes hanging loosely in his hand—not the least of which being that he was a cop and she was responsible for the death of her husband's mistress. Although she couldn't imagine herself being capable of murder, that it was an accident—and one she could not even remember—sounded implausible even to her own ears. Images of her half-dozen arrests as a juvenile flashed through her head, the humiliation and publicity. Her antics then would look like jaywalking in comparison to a murder trial. She wanted to tell him, wished she could trust him, but John was right. No one would believe her.

For Mason to believe her, the only way to get him out of her life, she would have to convince him that she trusted him. Completely. Only when she lifted her gaze to his did she realize her crying had stopped.

"Yes," she said.

"Take off your clothes, my pet." He tossed the ropes on the bed. "I'm going to check on that door."

She trembled as she shed her clothes, more from fear of herself than anything she thought Mason would do to her. She *did* trust him not to harm her physically. She just couldn't trust him with the truth. Her true fear, though, was that she would somehow give herself away. He was a skilled detective, after all, and she was no actress.

After an interminable length of time, he walked back with his phone on his ear and came to an abrupt halt at the sight of her standing naked beside the bed.

"Uh-huh," he said into his cell. "Thanks for calling." He turned off his phone and returned his focus to her. "God, you're beautiful."

Under different circumstances, she would have appreciated the compliment and probably even been aroused by his lengthy assessment, but now she just wanted to get this over with.

He removed his jacket and holster and laid them on the dresser. "Lie down on the bed," he said as he walked toward the headboard. "Move over to the middle, head on the pillows. That's right." As she carried out his directions, her heart thudded against her chest so hard, pulsating in her ears, she thought he must hear it as well. He took her left wrist and stretched it up at an angle. "Is that comfortable?" She nodded. He took the first length of rope and tied her wrist to the headboard with expert precision. Now she knew where this was headed.

As Mason tied her right wrist as he had the left, her heartbeats and breaths quickened, the silk ropes setting off an electric tickle between her legs. He pushed the covers down then tied her ankles to the footboard, spread-eagled, leaving her fully open to his perusal. And completely aroused. She lifted her head to see what he was doing. He stood in the center at the foot of the bed admiring his handiwork. As she laid her head back, she wondered if he could see how turned on she was, the very image of which made her nipples tighten and her clit tremble.

"Are you comfortable, my pet?"

After a succession of shallow breaths, she huffed out, "Yes."

He stepped around and sat on the bed beside her right arm, and she twisted her neck to look at him. "Yes what?"

"Yes, Sir."

He smiled. "Very good."

What was he going to do? Just sit there and stare at her? He hadn't even undressed yet. Her breasts ached for his hands, her nipples for his mouth. This was his torture. The more he sat there *not* touching her, the more she wanted him—*needed* him. Then he did touch her, but not how she wanted. He brushed the hair off of her forehead. *Why couldn't he brush those fingers lower—quite a bit lower?*

"What are you doing?" Alicia asked when she saw the blindfold.

"Shhh...No questions, my pet."

He positioned the blindfold over her eyes, sending her into darkness as her heart climbed into her throat. The combination of lust and terror wrapped around her tighter than the ropes. Then she remembered. *Apple.* Yes, she could say apple at any time and end this. The thought calmed her, and she relaxed into her bondage.

"I'm going in the other room for just a minute," he

said. "I'll be right back."

Wait. He's leaving me? Panic rose from her belly, her breathing harsh and fast now, and fear burning behind her eyes. She hadn't thought of that. He could leave her here like this, vulnerable, just walk out at any time. No one might find her for days. Or worse, someone *would* find her, naked and splayed out like a piglet on a spit.

"I'm here, my pet." He had returned as silently as he had gone. Damn that carpet. "You still doing OK?" he asked as he sat on the bed.

Say it now! Say apple! Make this stop! No, why would she? How long had he even been gone? Less than a minute? She just had to humor him a while longer and then…*Chitty Chitty, Bang Bang.*

She smiled. "Yes. Sir." Yes, she would just lie back and think of *Chitty Chitty, Bang Bang.*

"Good," he said, a laugh in his voice. "It's nice to see you smile." He stroked her hair, lighting a fuse that burned straight to her womb. *Could a safety word be used in reverse to get him to* start *doing something?*

"Is…is there anything I can do for *you*, Sir?"

"You appear to be rather tied up at the moment."

"Yes, but you seem to have me positioned in such a way that…I think we could manage."

"I thought you didn't want sex, my pet," he said, a slight edge to his voice.

"Can't a girl change her mind, Sir?"

The mattress shifted as he stood. "I have to step outside for a few minutes to make a call. We can talk about it when I come back."

"You're leaving again?"

"I'll be back in a few minutes."

Now she'd done it. She'd pissed him off by suggesting sex. Did he really have to make a phone call *now*? Who was so important that he had to call on a Sunday night and leave her naked and tied up like this? Her anxiety increased with every minute that passed and every scenario that ran through her head that led her back to the same conclusion. There was no call. He had just used that as an excuse to leave her. He might be gone for hours, if he ever came back.

His weight sank into the bed beside her. "I'm here, my pet," he said softly. With his thumbs, he wiped away the tears she didn't even know she had shed. "Why are you crying?"

She sniffled. "I-I don't know."

"Can I do anything for you to make you more comfortable?"

"Y-yes. I'm cold. Could you please put the covers over me, Sir?"

"Of course."

She was surprised at how he so readily agreed to her request. Although she was a little cold, the last time he had left her alone, her nudity disconcerted her, cold shame dousing her hot desire.

"There. Better?" he asked as he tucked the covers over her chest."

"Yes. Thank you, Sir."

He took his place on the bed beside her again. "Did you still want to discuss sex?" She said nothing. "You were sad when I came back, so I think you might have changed your mind again."

"Yes, Sir."

"If this is the end—of us—then I think that's better. Don't you agree?"

The end. The words nearly choked her. She didn't want it to be the end. They were just beginning.

"I have another question for you," he said when she failed to answer the last. "Do you know what DOC is?"

DOC? What was he asking her about now? DOC. DOC. How the hell did she know? DOC. First he asked her about the Department of Defense and now what? Department of Commerce? Department of—

She gasped, and her cheeks bloomed with fire. "D-Department of Corrections?"

He stood up and she would have sworn he stifled a laugh. "Yes, very good, my pet. The Department of Corrections. I have to step outside again. I'll be back in a few minutes."

From the moment he had tied the first rope, she had forgotten why she was allowing herself to be tied up to begin with. Her present situation had pushed aside all thoughts of Heidi and John and guilt and incarceration. Maybe he *had* been making phone calls. Maybe he had found out the truth. Now he was just toying with her, using the veiled threat of the Department of Corrections to coerce a confession out of her.

But it would be coercion. Anything he got out of her while tied naked and blindfolded couldn't be used in court, and he would know that.

This had nothing to do with getting a confession. What did he say? *Trust, honesty, and communication.* She had certainly never had that with John. She was surprised she had even trusted John enough to have him help her dispose of a body. Of course, what choice would she have had?

Why hadn't she just called the police right then when it happened? She wanted so badly to remember that night. She could see Heidi in the window, agitated, arguing with someone. She tried to suck the image from her subconscious. She could see them in the window now, Heidi arguing with John. No, it wasn't Heidi. That was the night she saw John arguing with Jude. Damn it, her thoughts were getting all muddled. She could clearly recall when they put the duffel bag with Heidi's body into the trunk, but she pictured it from a distance, like an out of body experience, astral projection.

She had kneeled and cried beside the girl's body even as they buried her. If she had been so torn up with guilt that she wanted to kill herself, why wouldn't she have confessed first? Given that poor girl's parents some closure and allowed them to have a proper burial.

And why in holy hell would she have opened that 2010 Château Lafite even in her sleep?

She needed help. She needed answers.

She needed Mason.

Alicia's fingertips caressed the silk ropes holding her to the bed, but instead of restraints, she thought of them as anchors, holding her down to Earth, providing her with the stability she so desperately needed.

She *did* trust Mason. He would help her. He would take care of her and protect her.

When would he be back? He'd been gone a long time this time. *Please come back*, she thought as she wept, the tears flowing down her cheeks and neck.

"He'll be back soon," she whispered, soothing herself. "He'll be back soon."

His hand came to rest on her forehead as he sat on the bed. "Alicia," he said, as soft as a cloud, like she might be sleeping and he didn't want to wake her. "Alicia."

A convulsive sob ran through her as he brushed away her tears. "Mason, you're back."

"I never left you," he said and pulled the blindfold from her eyes. "I was here with you the whole time. I never even left the room."

"Then why?"

"I want you to know you can trust me. You had to know I wouldn't abandon you like your mother or neglect you like your father or betray you like your husband." His words provoked a fresh onset of tears. "I will always take care of you. I will always be there for you when you need me." He held her head in his hands and laid kisses on her eyes, cheeks, and lips then gazed down at her. "If that's what you want."

"I do. I do trust you. I have to tell you something though. I...I think I killed Heidi."

He remained calm and said nothing for several moments as she held her breath through several quavering sobs.

"It was an accident, Mason."

"Why do you think you killed Heidi?"

"I-I went to confront her the night of my accident. John said I called him in hysterics because I had pushed her and she'd fallen and hit her head."

"John *told* you this, then. So you don't remember."

"I remember bits and pieces, fragments, like going

over there and John helping me put her body in the trunk, and..." She had to force the next words through her tears. "I remember her body lying there in the grass by the lake as we were burying her."

Mason pushed himself off the bed and turned his back on her, and she wondered if she had lost him after all. "And your accident?"

"John said after we buried her, I was so racked with guilt, I drove into the lake trying to kill myself."

"A-ha!" He rushed back to her side. "He's lying! Your airbag never deployed. Your car had to have rolled into the lake. That doesn't sound like a very efficient method of suicide."

"Then why would he—Oh, my God!" Her eyes widened as comprehension dawned as bright as a new day.

"Yes, *he* killed Heidi."

"What about the parts I remember?"

"You must have followed him. You saw what he was doing. He must have clubbed you over the head with something and pushed you in your car into the lake."

"He tried to kill me?"

"Yes, and I'm sure he's the one who's been terrorizing you all week. Let me get you out of these restraints." He began working on the first rope.

"But how could he? He doesn't have a key, and I changed the alarm code."

"I don't know, but he's the one who drugged you, too. You didn't stumble on some old X in your sleep. DOC isn't just the Department of Corrections. That's who called before. Your blood test showed you had the psychedelic Dimetho-something-or-other. DOC.

You'd never even heard of it. Damn this knot."

They both froze at a noise echoing in the other room, and Mason brought his index finger to his lips.

"He must be back," he said just above a whisper.

"Wouldn't he have seen your car?"

"I moved it into your neighbors' garage while you were getting undressed." He grabbed his holster and jacket from the dresser. "I'll be right in the closet. Don't do anything."

What did he think she would do? He disappeared into the dark closet but left the door open two inches.

Mason had loosened the rope on her left wrist, and she tried to work it free as her heart raced and her palms began to sweat.

"Alicia!" John cried out from the doorway. "Good God! What happened? Who did this to you?" With his long stride, he reached the bedside in four steps. He studied her bound wrists but made no move to untie her.

"John, what are you doing here?"

"I told you I'd come back tonight. Thank God I did."

"No, you told me to call you when I woke up."

"What difference does that make now?"

"How did you get in?"

"The front door, the same way as your attacker. Looks like he kicked it in. Or was there more than one?"

"Uh, no, only one. Could you untie me? Or maybe you should call 911 first."

"Tell me who did this to you. Did you get a good look at him?" He fiddled with the rope a moment then said, "I think it would be easier if I cut them off. I'll get a knife from the kitchen." As he walked out of the room, she realized he had tightened the knot rather than loosening it.

He left her there for several minutes then returned with the largest, sharpest knife she owned. "You were gone a long time," she said. "Did you call the police?"

"No, it took me a while to find a knife I thought would do the trick." He stopped midway into the bedroom and leaned against the dresser, studying the knife.

"The rope isn't that thick, John."

"Tell me, dear, did he rape you?"

"What? No."

"Oh. Well, let's hope he left some other physical evidence for the police."

"What are you waiting for? Are you going to untie me or what?"

"I just think it would be better for the police to find you like this, for the crime scene. It might give them some clues."

"Didn't you notice anything unusual in the kitchen?"

"What do you mean?"

"When you got the knife. Didn't you notice something strange in the kitchen that might help the police *investigation*?" He drew his brows together and shook his head. "The wine glasses, John. Someone poured wine into all of the glasses."

His face turned red, but then he chuckled. "I assumed you'd just been acting out your guilt again."

"You mean *your* guilt."

The smile fell from his face. "You're awfully

brazen considering your current predicament."

"You're going to kill me anyway. Aren't you? Like you did Heidi?"

He blew out a world-weary sigh, like murder just wasn't as easy as it used to be. "I didn't want to kill you, Alicia. I've done everything I could to avoid it. If you hadn't been following me that night in the first place, none of this would have happened."

"I saw you arguing with her."

"Yes. She wanted us to go away together, and the night before we were supposed to leave, I told her I wasn't going, admitted I'd never planned to go. I didn't want to kill her, but she gave me no choice. She threatened to tell everyone, ruin my chances at tenure. So I strangled her. It was practically self-defense."

The calmness with which he described taking the life of this girl, literally *killing for tenure*, caused acid to rise in her throat. This man—her *husband*—with whom she had shared love and a home and a life, and she'd never really known him at all.

"And then what happened? I caught you burying Heidi's body, so you hit me over the head and tried to drown me?"

"I didn't want to have to do that. I do love you, Alicia. I always have. When you found me burying her, I just reacted and hit you with the shovel. I was so relieved when you woke up with no memory of any of it."

"Then why this whole production—hiding things? Writing on the mirror? Drugging me?"

"Because you insisted on calling the police about Daniel Holloman. I tried to talk you out of it. I told you he was fine, but you always think you're right about everything! Then when you described someone dragging a duffel bag into the trunk, I knew you were starting to remember that night. And you see the lengths I have gone to *not* to kill you? I could have killed you any of the times I've been in here. I just tried to discredit you so if you ever *did* remember anything, no one would believe you. You wouldn't even trust yourself."

And he'd almost succeeded. "So why do you have to kill me now?"

"Because you've got that detective snooping around and sniffing up your skirts, and you're remembering more and more and talking about going to the police and telling them everything. And lo and behold, I get here, and the job's half done! Someone's already broken in and tied you up." He set down the knife and pulled medical gloves from his pocket. "Slitting your throat will be the easy part."

As he snapped the gloves on, she asked, "How did you do it? How did you sneak into the house without a key or triggering the alarm or anyone seeing your car?"

"You forgot the garage door opener." He picked up the knife and approached her with a grin. "Without a car, you never had a reason to go through the mudroom; so when I was here last week, I unlocked the door to the garage and disconnected it from the security system."

"Turn around and drop the knife," Mason said from the closet doorframe. He had his gun raised and aimed at John, who didn't move. "Go ahead, Meador. I'd love an excuse to shoot you."

To Alicia's bitter disappointment, John dropped the knife and turned around. "What are you doing here, Crawley?"

"Didn't you want to find the man who broke in and tied up Alicia?"

After agonizing hours at the station giving multiple statements, Alicia and Mason returned to the house on Lilac Lane in the early morning hours for the second day in a row. He pushed the front door open without unlocking it.

"I'm afraid your door is seriously fucked," he said as they stumbled in.

"Yes, the mysteries may be solved, but the mess remains." She wobbled into the kitchen and began pouring wine down the drain. "All my beautiful Bordeaux," she said with an air of melancholy.

He took the glass out of her hand and set it aside, and she dropped her forehead against his sternum.

"I'm not leaving you here alone again until we get the lock on that door fixed."

"OK," she said in a childlike voice.

"Look at me, Alicia." She lifted her head and gazed at him with those beautiful, bloodshot, dark chocolate eyes and rested her chin on his chest, and he wrapped his arms around her. "I need to know. Are we doing this?"

"Doing what?"

"Our relationship. Are you ready for this? To be my submissive?"

"I want to. I'd like to try, but…"

His muscles tensed reflexively. "But what?"

"We only met a few days ago. Yes, we have incredible sexual chemistry, but we don't know anything about each other."

He smiled and kissed the tip of her nose. "We're starting out with trust, honesty, and communication. That's the hard part. Some couples don't have that after a lifetime together. Getting to know each other—*that* will be the fun part."

She smiled and lifted her face to press her lips against his.

"Now, come, my pet," he said. "I'm taking you to bed."

"Yes, Sir."

The end

○

If you enjoyed *Alicia's Possession*, you will love:

DEADLINE
by Scarlet Hawthorne

HE WANTS HER BODY AND HEART,
BUT A KILLER WANTS HER SOUL...

After her erotic romance novels become international bestsellers, writer Gillian Tate cannot enjoy her long-sought success once her husband files for divorce and she becomes the target of threats from a religious fringe hate group. When she tries to find peace in the solitude of a remote lakeside cabin to complete the third novel in the trilogy, not only does she meet the man who can fulfill her own secret desires, she also discovers she hasn't escaped danger by leaving the city.

When the Adirondack town's police chief Sam Taylor learns of the threats and checks in on the notorious author, he is surprised to find the voluptuous woman he meets is nothing like he would have imagined from her erotic novels - but everything he has imagined in his own fantasies

Can he and the woman of his dreams escape her waking nightmare?

ADULT CONTENT: This erotic romantic suspense includes bondage between consenting adults.

OTHER TITLES BY COLETTE SAUCIER

Pulse and Prejudice
The Confession of Mr. Darcy, Vampire

In this thrilling and sensual adaptation of the classic love story, Elizabeth Bennet and the citizens of Hertfordshire know Fitzwilliam Darcy to be a proud, unpleasant sort of man, but they never suspect the dark secret of his true nature. He is not a man at all – but a vampire.

When the haughty and wealthy Fitzwilliam Darcy arrives in the rural county of Hertfordshire, he finds he cannot control his attraction to Elizabeth Bennet – a horrifying thought because, as she is too far below his social standing to ignite his heart, he fears she must appeal to the dark impulses he struggles to suppress.

Set against the vivid backdrop of historical Regency England, this adaptation of *Pride and Prejudice* follows the cursed Mr. Darcy as he endeavours to overcome both his love and his bloodlust for Miss Elizabeth Bennet. Although *Pulse and Prejudice* adheres to the original plot and style of the Jane Austen classic, it is neither a "mash-up" nor "fan fiction" but an imaginative, thrilling variation told primarily from Mr. Darcy's point of view as he descends into the seedier side of London and introduces Elizabeth to a world of passion and the paranormal she never knew existed.

Dearest Bloodiest Elizabeth
Book II: The Confession of Mr. Darcy, Vampire

Set me as a seal upon thine heart,
as a seal upon thine arm:
for love is strong as death;
jealousy is cruel as the grave.
     Song of Solomon 8:6

In this lurid, lusty sequel to *Pulse and Prejudice*, death shadows the newlywed Darcys from Pemberley to the parlors of Regency London to the courtyards of Antebellum New Orleans. As Elizabeth discovers the trials and travails of marriage to a vampire, can Darcy ever believe that she loves him as he is? Or will his jealousy tear them apart?

This is the sequel to *Pulse and Prejudice*; however, as it is not an Austen adaptation, the reader will find it darker, bloodier, and more provocative than Book 1.

Cartel Widow

"When truth is buried underground it grows, it chokes, it gathers such an explosive force that on the day it bursts out, it blows up everything with it." – Émile Zola, *J'accuse*

In this thrilling romantic noir suspense, DEA agent David Alvarez invested four years in deep undercover infiltrating the ruthless Sonora Drug Cartel only to have his primary target gunned down by a rival gang. Now his only hope in salvaging the operation and bringing the largest drug trafficker in the world to justice lies with the man's beautiful, young widow Catherine, whom he cannot bring himself to trust.

Drowning in wine and despair, Catherine would do anything to break free from the clutches of the cartel; but despite her desperate efforts, she can never escape the mistakes of her past that continue to haunt her.

Even though he cannot deny their mystical, mutual attraction, David must carry out his orders – from both the DEA and the Cartel – catching Catherine in a spider web of duplicity and deceit. How far will David go to bring down the cartel? If he succeeds in winning the widow's trust, would he be willing to risk her life – or his heart?

NOTE: This is a *noir* romantic suspense. Contains strong language and intense sexual situations appropriate for the genre..

SPECIAL BONUS

Alicia Embracing the Dark

There are many ways to be haunted, not all of them supernatural. From photo albums to love letters, the memory of bad choices, broken promises, lost loves, and shattered dreams can often linger for longer than the glow of satisfaction from our greatest accomplishments. Indeed, the most frightening ways to be haunted may be in the many ways we haunt ourselves. – Tonya Hurley, from *ghostgirl: Lovesick*

A dark anthology by Alicia Pageant, the heroine of *Alicia's Possession*.

Three vignettes written in the aftermath of her husband's infidelity and her disillusionment with romantic relationships, Alicia's own depression and despair resonates through the characters she has created to express the desolation no one else can see.

Alicia Embracing the Dark

Alicia Pageant

Second Edition, November 1, 2013
Southern Girl Press
www.southerngirlpress.com

Editor: Colette L. Saucier

DEDICATION

To Stephanie.

FOREWARD

Although certainly not as stigmatized as in the past, even today, with 350 million people struggling with it worldwide and as the leading cause of disability, depression remains a silent, shameful secret to most who deal with it on a daily basis. Those who have never experienced depression find it difficult—if not impossible—to understand.

This trio of vignettes is intended to express some aspect of depression as experienced by the author at some point in her life. It is published collectively under the name of a fictional character, selected because she suffers from major depressive disorder and suicidal thoughts in the wake of her collapsing marriage in her own story, in which depression is a primary motif.

SPIRITS

The door caught for a moment before she pushed it open and stumbled into the dark. "Ah, here we are," she said, switching on the lamp.

"So this is where you live," he said, closing the door and bolting it. "I've seen it quite a few times from the road. I always thought it looked haunted."

"Oh, but it is! Spirits!" she called out as she glided about the room. "Spirits…ah, friendly spirits." She pulled a bottle of Canadian Club from behind a small bar. "Spirits to raise the spirits. Join me?"

"Thank you, no. I think we've both had enough, but if you're still, uh, thirsty, please go ahead."

She splashed an inch of clear brown liquid into a short glass, neat. "Drinking alone doesn't bother me; but, mind you, in the morning when you're wanting a hair from the dog, it will all be gone – I having drunk it."

"Was that an invitation?"

"Was what? Oh, never mind. Don't try to decipher some meaning from my words when I've had a tad too much fun." She strolled over to him and put her arms on his shoulders, clasping her glass behind his neck with both hands. "But there's so much more fun to be had." She kissed him gently several times on the lips then turned and dropped heavily onto the sofa. "Come. Sit. Stay." But rather than sitting beside her, he took the seat opposite. "It's been awhile. Hasn't it? Not since last July, since Francis threw that ridiculous – what was the theme? – yes, that dreadful Bastille Day party, almost as bad as tonight's gala affair…no, July was worse."

"Yes, July," he said thoughtfully, his gaze cast beyond her, with a smile. "That was a *hot* month. Wasn't it?"

She threw her head back and laughed, spilling some of her drink on her silk shift. "Good for you! Not so for others less fortunate."

"Yourself?" he asked.

"There are millions – no, billions of people in the world, a majority of whom, I'm sure, are less fortunate than yourself."

"So?"

"So why pick on me?" She clumsily gathered herself off the couch and headed toward the bar.

"You're drunk."

"You're right...No, actually, I'm quite sober. There comes a time in people's lives – well, some people's lives...in my life at least – when sobriety and inebriation are so similar that, from the outside, no one can tell the difference; the reason being that one's state of drunkenness is closer to sobriety than the state of being sober. Is. But I assume it all depends on the state of mind – or the state of Maine."

"I believe you are deep in the state of inebriation – as well as denial."

"But you don't know me at all, now. Do you? You only know what you perceive, and you only see what I allow you to see. This could all be an act." She gulped from the glass.

He stood and reached for her drink. "You're drinking too much too quickly."

Pulling her hand away from his grasp, she said, "You're just being selfish. Aren't you? Thinking of that morning dog hair? Yes, I suppose that is an invitation. Or not so much an invitation as a confirmation of what we both assumed would occur this evening."

"You weren't like this last July."

"Oh, that wasn't me. Or I, rather. That was my twin cousin Josephine. Didn't you find her terribly attractive?"

"No, no, no."

"You didn't find her attractive?"

"No. I mean, yes, I find her attractive; but, no, you don't have a twin cousin – or any twin for that matter. I think I will have that drink."

"All right, you caught me in a lie: It was I in July. But we barely spoke. So how could you know what I was like last summer?"

He fumbled through the bottles behind the bar, and – aside from a filthy fifth of crème de menthe – finding all of them nearly empty. "What has happened since then? Whether we spoke or not, you were not like this."

She flopped onto the couch and set her drink on the end table beside. "Do you really think it's any of your goddamn business?"

He stood straight and stiffened, forcing out his breath on a heavy sigh. "You're right, of course. I'm only trying to understand you."

"But if you did understand me, you would quickly lose interest. One only pursues that which he cannot understand. Therein lays the mystery."

"The mystery?"

"May it rest in peace…with the spirits."

He brushed the dust from the bottles from his hands. "Don't you have any vodka?"

"Stoli. In the fridge. You want it straight?" She pushed herself up from the sofa and staggered into the kitchen.

"Please." Alone, he glanced around the room. Neat enough but with many dust collectors – trinkets from thoughtless gifts – but by no means Dickensian. A red crocheted afghan hung across the back of the couch, and the coffee table was marred with white circles left by forgotten drinks. He spotted a laptop at rest on an inexpensive desk in the corner. He opened it and read words blinking on the document that filled the screen: "This moment was gone even before I had acknowledged its existence." He closed the computer.

"Here we are," she called out as she brought him his drink.

"Thanks." He took a short sip, admiring the burn as much as the taste. "How's your writing been?"

"Novel number three has been slow in coming. I hope that, when I do complete it, it will be publisher-approvable as well." They returned to their respective places on the couch and chair.

"What's your new book about?"

"About time. Wasted time. Wasted lives." Her mouth turned in a half-smile. "Did you read my other books?"

"Well, uh...."

"I know you. Of course you didn't."

"I've been...busy. I *wanted* to, but – "

"So why would care what my new novel is about?"

With a shrug, he said, "Just making conversation."

"My goodness, you haven't changed. Just the preliminary pleasantries before the main event."

"Look, I still care about you, just as much as I ever did."

"And that says it all. But back to my book – I'll tell you one thing whether you want to hear it or not. I think it could be my best if I could ever get it out of my head and onto the page."

"Is it autobiographical?"

"As much as fiction can be. But, on second thought, let's talk about something more interesting."

"What would you prefer?"

"Tell me what you've been up to."

"Me? Oh, I'm boring. I've just returned from Canada on business and – "

She cut him off. "Really? A dear friend of mine has just returned from there as well. George Bennett – did you see him there?"

"We're talking about an entire country! I'd have a better chance of running into him here."

"I suppose that's true."

"'A dear friend,' is he? I've never heard you mention him before. Is he new?"

"I did mention him to you, a long time ago. One night in bed. We had just finished making love – or fucking, or whatever it is that we do. Or did do. And quite well, I might add. I was telling you about something, I've forgotten what, and his name crossed my mind; and I said I would tell you about him someday."

"But you never did."

"You see there, you *do* remember!" She barked out a laugh, which died quickly. "Well, I would have told you if we hadn't…."

"Hadn't what?"

"Stopped *communicating*, so to speak."

"Is that what happened?"

"You tell me. Lord, it's been so long. How am I supposed to remember? Our on-again-off-again dance went on for so long, I wouldn't be able to say what finally ended it...stopped the music."

"Well...I'm here now."

"So you are. Where's my drink?" Her head fell to her shoulder and she spied her glass beside her and stood to freshen it.

"Have you become a lush?" he asked with his attention focused on the bottle as she poured.

"Certainly not!" She squinted at the drink in her hand, as if reconsidering. "Well, possibly. I suppose it depends on your definition of the word 'lush.'" She walked over to the desk and grabbed a dictionary from its position between other outdated reference books and blew the dust from its edge. "Let me see...'Having or characterized by luxuriant vegetation.'" She read on. "No, wait. 'Slang – a drunkard.' Yes, that fairly well defines me: The neighborhood lush and free-lance superhero living in a state of luxuriant vegetation."

"No, I don't think you are a lush."

"Well, you brought it up. So what *do* you think of me?"

He paused and took a slow sip from his drink. "A mystery."

She stared at him from across the room. "That's so silly and sweet for you to say. I would very much like to kiss you right now. I'm not going to, but I thought you might like to know I wanted to."

With eyebrows raised in her direction, he shook his head. "You are unreal."

"I am underrated, unattached, unhappy, unabashed, uninhibited, and unabridged, but I am undeniably real."

"Unhappy?"

"You're right. I'm not real. Not really. I told you this could all be an act. All the world a stage."

He brought his glass down onto the bar with a harsh thud. "Goddamnit, stop this! Stop playing these word games! Just talk to me!"

"I'm a writer. I love word games. Not Scrabble so much."

"Talk to me."

"What we had together, you and I...we had something nice."

"Now don't try to tell me I am the cause of your unhappiness. We stopped seeing each other seven years ago."

"Has it really been that long? Yes, I suppose it has. No, you have nothing to do with my becoming a lush, as you so eloquently put it; but even if you did, I wouldn't tell you. It would inflate your ego too much. No, no one did this to me. This road I chose on my own."

"But why?"

"Do you like this house?" She floated through the room. "It's not mine, actually. I'm house-sitting for a friend who is spending time abroad, but she's been gone nearly a year now. She went there to play nursemaid to her elderly grandmother, who was supposedly on her least breath; but the old lady keeps hanging on. My friend fears that if she came home, the minute her foot stepped through the door, the phone would ring and her grandmother would be dead. Not that the ringing phone would be the cause of death, but you know what I mean. I don't think she would be heartbroken by the call. On the contrary, I'd say she wishes the old bat would pass on so she could finally come home, but she couldn't live down the guilt of having abandoned her grandmother. I myself keep praying – figuratively speaking – that the old woman lives on and prospers into her hundreds. I don't want to lose my home. To think that my future depends on the life of an ailing old woman across the pond. I've never even met the grandmother, but I feel she and I share something. We both want her to live more than anything else in the world, I possibly even more than she."

She hadn't realized she'd turned her back to him until he came up behind her and rubbed her arms. She turned around and they kissed.

"Do you want me to stay?" he asked.

"Yes…for tonight."

She walked back to the couch and sat down, and he claimed the spot beside her.

"You know, I was married for a while," she said.

"That's what I was told, but I didn't see him at Francis's party, and you weren't with anyone tonight, so…"

"It ended that night. After the Bastille Day party."

"I…I'm sorry. Was there an argument? What happened?"

She smirked with a sniff. "No, there was no argument. It would have been less painful if we *had* fought. God knows I've had my share of pain since."

"Another woman?"

"No, I wish there'd been a physical object for my blame."

"Then what was it? Why did he leave you?"

She closed her eyes and leaned her head against the back of the couch and laughed softly. "I know what you're thinking. You think he left me because of my drinking."

"Is that what happened?"

She returned her eyes to him. "You silly boy. I left him."

I don't understand. Is this why you – "

"We were killing each other – death by stagnation. Like an abandoned swimming pool. We were married four years ago, when we couldn't afford to be. He's an attorney, you see – or I bet you can't see me with an attorney – and he was just starting out. And we fought constantly in that cramped, dank, little apartment – over money, bills, anything. Then he was offered a position at a law firm. And I sold my first novel, and then the second. We moved into a luxury apartment with a view. We had money, so we didn't have money problems. There was nothing left to fight about. For the first time, I realized arguing had become our sole means of communication. I had no good reason to leave, but there was, likewise, no good reason to stay. I still loved him, I think – a little, at least – because I let it die in his sleep. No fights. No confrontations. No 'we can work it out' or 'give it one more chance.' A clean break. I left while he was out of town, in Washington. We had a short, uneventful divorce – just as our marriage had been."

"And that's why you get drunk?"

"You are laboring under a serious misconception. I don't drink to be drunk; I drink to be numb."

"Numb from what?"

"From disappointment. I don't have the time to waste *feeling* as sad as I am."

"But when did you start drinking like this? You never did before."

"I never knew I wanted to before."

"So when did it start?"

"Ah, if I unveil the mystery, you won't need to buy my new novel."

"I'm not going to buy it anyway."

"Touché. But, no, I'm not so inexperienced with alcohol as to congest tonight with maudlin melodrama. Although that *is* my style."

"I remember."

"Yes, I spent many hours crying on your shoulder in my youth when *tragedy* seemed a daily occurrence. You were always quite patient, although on occasion I distinctly remember hearing you snore."

His laugh sounded forced and blood crept into his cheeks. "I didn't mind. I cared about – "

"Blahblahblahblah. Words, words, words. How easily they trickle off the tongue like spittle. Don't be uncomfortable. I knew you before I brought you home with me. You're set for this evening. I'll satisfy your lust if not your mild curiosity."

"You're not fooling me. I think you *want* to talk about it."

"Perhaps I do, but I don't do everything I want to do. Unless it concerns alcohol." She slid from her seat on the sofa over to the bar where she drained the bottle of whisky. Noting the Canadian label, she said, "You never finished telling me about Canada."

"You interrupted me."

"Well, you were right. It was boring. That's why we stopped our dance. Outside of bed, we were both bored."

"I'm interested in you now."

"Why now? Because other people buy my books? Because I've brought this drizzle-dreary town some modest notoriety? What a shame you have to rely on the taste of others to define your interests."

"I don't think that's fair!"

"Neither do I."

"You're twisting everything."

"I have a twisted mind. Do you want another drink?"

He yawned. "No, I'm fine."

"I suppose that's supposed to be a subtle hint. Well, I'm not ready for bed yet. I'm overflowing with nervous energy. A shame I can't pour this into that keyboard. You aren't in a hurry. Are you?"

"So what are you going to do when your friend's grandmother dies?"

"First, I'll have a drink."

"I could have guessed that."

"Then I'll get my hands on some money and move on."

"What about the money from the sales of your books?"

"There's a little phrase used in the publishing world: Advance against royalties. Besides, anyone who wanted to buy my novels has already done so."

"Is there anyone you could stay with?"

"I certainly hope that is not an offer. No, no one

could stand living with me anymore. Nor can I imagine living with someone else. Drinking does have its disadvantages. One must be more discriminating in choosing companions. They must accept my drinking, which generally means they drink too much themselves. And who wants to be surrounded by a bunch of drunks?"

"You could stop drinking."

"And you could stop prying."

"Why won't you open up to me? What do you have to lose?"

"What do I have to gain? But you're right. You are the only one to whom I could reveal myself without the use of a pseudonym."

She took a swig of whisky and swished it around in her mouth before speaking. "Don't say I didn't warn you. Let us return to July. Shall we? Almost a year ago. I left Francis's party early, it was such a bore, especially with you tied up with your little coquette. My husband was in D.C., so I came home to an empty apartment and felt it – alone. You would have liked that apartment. I decorated it to your taste. Isn't it odd how you could still influence me? My husband never knew that, in a way, he was living in another man's apartment.

"So there I was, alone. As you've alluded to several times this evening, I had never been a heavy drinker; so the only thing we had with any alcoholic content was a few bottles of champagne, which had been residing in the vegetable bin of my refrigerator since New Year's Eve. That's a fair assessment of how much we'd had to celebrate in seven months. Or had had vegetables, for that matter. I put a couple of CDs in the player, popped open a bottle, and began to drink – and I didn't stop.

"I guess I was, as you say, drinking too much too quickly, or my tolerance was just shot to shit, because the champagne started hitting me harder than I had remembered. Halfway through the first bottle, I began dipping my fingertip into the glass and spinning it around the rim of the flute – Imperial crystal, that's where my advance went – creating this high-pitched whistle that rang throughout the room. But I did it without thinking, as though my mind had been divided into two parts: One controlled my actions and the garbled things that occasionally fell out of my mouth, and the other controlled my thoughts and merely observed the rest of me as if a separate entity. Once I had polished off the first bottle, I realized I was playing with my hands. I noticed this as a stranger acknowledges an autistic child. I was no longer in control of my actions or what I….In any case, I was drunk.

"A warm tingling filled my legs, and I felt dizzy, much like I do now. The second CD ended, so I wobbled over and set the music on shuffle, which turned out to be quite a challenge! My second mind willed the first to act normally, control my motor skills, but it wouldn't have it. I am not a person to wobble – thank God no one could see me! No, I wish he could have seen me." She waved the last words away. "Oh, that's just drunk talk. If he had seen me, he'd have thought me a fool. I *was* a fool. No one gets drunk for such a poor excuse unless he has no excuse at all. We hadn't gotten into a fight. He hadn't cheated on me or hit me. I know you're disappointed. It was nothing dramatic. There was no catharsis that pushed me over the edge. I was just lonely. And not because he was out of town. I saw people, was with people, but not him. Not really. The apartment felt vacant even when he was there. For once, I wished I were promiscuous, although sex was not what I really wanted, needed so desperately; but I'd take what I could get. I was so lonely, lonely, lonely.

"Are you enjoying this gossip? Don't fall asleep yet. Your ego will enjoy this. I decided to call you. Not sure what made me decide to do that. Wait, yes I do. It was the song that came on − 'our' song. Not actually 'our' song, but the song I always thought of as ours. You know the one. Seeing you at the party for the first time in years, and we had barely spoken, just the formalities, like strangers. I started to call you before realizing your number had probably changed, then figured you were more than likely still at the party. And you had a date.

"I don't remember what happened to the second bottle of champagne, but my head grew so heavy, I had a difficult time holding it above my shoulders. So I went to the bedroom and stretched out across the unmade bed, staring at the light fixture in the ceiling. I had never before noticed alcohol causing my ears to clog, and I tried to yawn them open. The music in the next room called to me as if from far away. Such sad music. I began to cry for perhaps the seventh time since popping the first bottle. My eyes were burning already, but that second brain could only observe the absurdity of the situation, laughing at the fool. A song I loved drifted in from the other room. The singer's voice was husky, and I wished he were singing about me. I wished that he were there with me. Who was it? Oh, it doesn't matter. Not knowing his name made it possible for him to be anyone. Even you. Even him. Except he doesn't have a husky voice. And he would never say those things, speak those words to me. Unless he were drunk. Like me.

"I lay there thinking about my life for what I suppose must have been hours, but the only evidence of the passing of time was the progression of the music. I like not feeling time moving on – another divine reason to drink. Then it was morning. I wasn't even aware of the transition or recalled having slept, but the light from dawn spilled in and over me. I got up, drank some juice, straightened up from my solitary drinking. Then I packed a suitcase, left a note, and checked into a hotel.

"I know you think I was wallowing in self-pity, and I was. That's one of the things I enjoy about drinking. When I'm sober, I have to remain strong, independent. It is considered undignified to be weak, to need someone. What kind of feminist would that make me? You probably won't believe this, but I don't get drunk every night. Sometimes I forget to drink for days. But then, inevitably, the disappointment and desperation start getting to me, and I take advantage of the loophole that allows a grown woman to make a fool of herself."

They were both silent a long time, staring into their drinks.

"You're not saying anything," she said. "Do I disgust you?"

He frowned and shook his head. "No. I just don't get it. I guess I don't understand."

"Haven't you ever been desperate with longing for anything in your entire life?"

He thought a moment then said, "No, I guess I haven't."

"Then forget self-pity. I feel sorry for *you*."

She set her drink aside and sidled over to where he sat on the sofa and offered him both her hands. He stood and kissed her, softly at first but then deepening in that warm familiar way.

"Do you want to go to bed?" he asked.

"Yes, let's go to bed," she said as they turned toward the stairs, "and I won't change your life, and you won't change mine. And I promise not to write you into my book."

PORTRAIT IN STILL LIFE

A child of fourteen, Catherine could not fully appreciate the effect her mother's death had on her father, on the filament of his belief system. At the funeral, he had managed to shake the hands of blank-faced strangers and give spoken thanks for their sympathy but nothing more, finding conversation unwieldy.

The pain in his expression revealed grief heavily imbued with guilt. He possessed an arrogance, an ironic hubris, that *he* had been the cause of her death.

The seeds of this idée fixe had first taken root when their son had been killed in the car accident for which he alone was at fault. From then on, he watched in impotent suspense as his wife faded away, her sorrow an ally to her illness in its ruthless pillage of her life.

Once alone, Catherine having gone with her grandparents and the others returning to their lives, he collapsed upon their marriage bed still in his mourning suit and lay motionless on his side, staring at the wall. He never broke his gaze, through light and darkness, as the sun set and rose through the window behind him, for five days. His appearance, thin and grey in his crumpled suit, shocked Catherine when her grandmother brought her home. His mother chastised him for his selfishness, admonishing him for not being strong for his daughter. He gaped at her from the living room chair where he had been deposited. Although her grandmother urged Catherine to return with her, the girl insisted that she remain with her father.

Catherine would rise earlier than before, preparing breakfast then heading to school. In the evenings, she cooked dinner and told her father about her day. He would pick at his food and respond to her in low, gravely monosyllables. His torpor forced Catherine into action. She called his office, requested an extended leave; and when she came home to her father sitting in darkness because the power had been shut off, she began forging his signature on checks to pay bills. And all the while, her father felt justified in his depression.

Catherine's words to him ranged from patronizing

cheerfulness to outrage and fury. "Talk to me!" she would scream at his anguished stare. "This isn't fair! I miss her, too. She was my mother. I need you. I need you!" Reaching a quavering falsetto, she fell to her knees before him and cried into his lap. His eyes dropped to his weeping daughter, but he could not bring a hand to her head to comfort her. He could only superficially register the pain of anyone other than himself, all empathy buried alongside his wife.

The sadness had swallowed him. In his mind, his existence – and in a sense, existence in general – before he and his wife had met had only occurred to prepare him for his life with her. Without this, he had no purpose, no future. He had ceased to exist.

In her, he recognized every quality for which he found himself lacking: the irreverence and self-assurance that could only develop through authenticity, being truly in touch with oneself. And this she gave to him, the ability to break free from the restraints of lifelong conditioning and awaken the dormant passions within his soul. But once she had opened the door to this passage, he closed himself off from a certain sphere of reality.

Controlled by his new-found freedom, he subjected himself to the scrutiny and wrath of others by vocalizing his values and beliefs with volume and fervent confidence – no topic too insignificant for an opinion – never allowing logic or sentiment to infringe on his infallibility, found the road to Damascus.

He regarded his marriage through that same lens. Nothing could convince him that he was not the first and only to experience such great love. Further, he considered it essential for all to know the joy they shared, to envy the completion he had achieved with her. He held her close not as a trophy but as a savior. The taste of her tongue would illicit such ecstatic insight, with each embrace he became ever more certain that he alone knew this supreme devotion, which no other creature could possibly attain.

When she would roll her eyes at him and, at times, complain that he crowded her, he knew that even she – the sheerest, brightest light of his life – could not understand. Occasionally he would sulk at abiding alone in the experience, being misunderstood; but some amount of suffering must be expected in exchange for this ultimate, complete and perfect love.

The children were incidental, merely evidence that he had lain with this woman. He lacked the capacity to anticipate the tragic effect of the loss of a child, and he watched on in horror as his wife grew ill with grief, clinging to her daughter as if to save her remaining child from harm. He wept as well, bitter tears of fear that his negligence had loosened his grasp, feeling her slip through his fingers. The icon of his devotion pulled away from the eyes of the world, he would suffer the tragedy of his own making. Only *he* had known this perfect love, and he alone had destroyed it.

Now he stared at nothing, recalling her face and the warmth of her body, remembering every moment together as an event of historic proportion. These memories not only served as an urn for the cremains of his life; they were the epicenter of all existence.

Recognizing that he neglected his daughter did nothing to motivate him or improve his mental state; indeed, it contributed to its disintegration. As time passed, his belief in the paralyzing effect of his grief evolved into a vise restraining him, penetrating him with inertia. He witnessed the pain it provoked in Catherine but did not respond, as if any acknowledgement of her sense of loss might diminish his own. And yet, knowing that she suffered enhanced his guilt until it rendered him unworthy of her love and respect.

Had he believed in a higher power, perhaps he could have allowed himself to share the blame with some grand design, but he had faith in nothing but himself. Unable to conceive of a conscious being manipulating human destiny, he alone controlled his fate and, thus, the suffering that surrounded and consumed him. His guilt conceived in arrogance validated the newly-divined essence of his evil nature; feeding, nursing, nurturing his certainty, tolerating no dissension. He encouraged Catherine's disdain, willed her not to bestow upon him the love he did not deserve.

The cycle of his condition continued until emotion replaced all thought, and he merely wallowed in guilt and self-pity. He sat alone in the dark in self-fulfilling autism, no longer even a presence in the room but a slight object unaware of its surrounding.

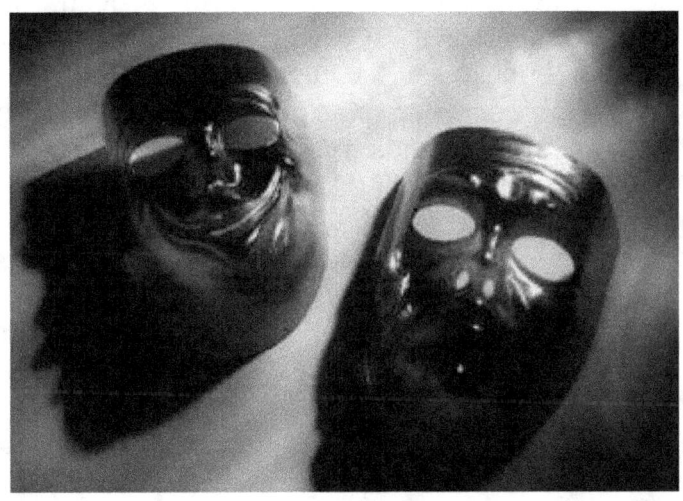

DÉNOUEMENT

And so our hero and heroine find it necessary to bring their relationship to an end and write their lives on different pages from then on. They both mourn, not so much because it was ending but because it had been based on lies. And the truth frightened them.

For our heroine is actually the antagonist of this story. She pursued a course of action for which she had a reasonable expectation of tragic results – especially if the hero were sincere in his devotion. In reality, our heroine was not in love with him. She had admitted love was not an accurate description of her feelings, which were neither equivalent nor equal to "love" but something quite separate and apart. She chose to use the term "I am you" for a significant reason.

Which brings us to the question of motive: Why would our heroine pursue an avenue that allowed the hero to believe she did, in fact, love him? The point may seem obvious. The heroine wanted desperately for the hero to be in love with her, which one might consider odd since she did not harbor those emotions in return. Although not her original design (and, in fact, she began with no intention at all), this desire for him to love her quickly became an inherent force in her behavior, the tragic flaw in her character being the belief that she must have a man's affection to have value. She pursued his love under the assumption that it could restore her sense of self-worth, and the knowledge that our hero might be hurt by her actions in no way deterred her from that quest. Once having sworn her love and demanding he do the same, the first requirement for our tragedy had been fulfilled.

Our story takes a dramatic turn with our hero's untimely anagnorisis when he realizes this is not love. Lying on the floor, the heroine beneath him with her face stinging and tears streaming from her eyes, he screams at her from two inches, demanding to know why she is doing this. Again she swears she loves him, but by now he suspects and is determined to force it out of her. She protests her innocence – the sincerity of her devotion – and he is subdued but not convinced. He had touched on the truth, and it could not be erased from his consciousness. He had now reached the peripeteia, necessary for the remaining sequence of events leading to our conclusion.

The question remains as to why, even once directly confronted, our heroine did not confess to the true nature of her intentions. She would prefer to convince herself she had done so to protect his feelings; but in truth she merely lacked courage. For one, she could not admit to him that which she tried to deny to herself – she had deceived him with purely selfish motives and no regard for his well-being – believing that such an admission would prove once and for all that she is, in fact, a villain, as she had suspected for some time. And secondly, if not more importantly, she feared a confession would insure the loss of her hero's love, which of course had been her primary objective.

Thus, the relationship took a dramatic downturn culminating in the tragic climax that confirmed the affair, relationship, friendship were dead. But the truth goes beyond even this, for our heroine – although undoubtedly the hubristic character in our tale – should not be held entirely in scorn. Essentially, she had been accurate in her statement, "I am you." Just as she did not love our hero, neither did he love her. Although perhaps not aware of it at the time, he, too, had been motivated by the hope that, by securing the love of another, he could find validation and self-worth. He merely lacked the experience and self-awareness to differentiate that need from love.

The irony of our story comes from the fact that our hero and heroine were bleeding one another for something that their counterparts could not provide.

The only ones capable of defining their value were themselves, but this fact eluded them until the action had commenced.

Now having realized that the very people for whom they searched were, indeed, themselves, will our hero and heroine stab pins through their eyes and roam the world in blind misery? Our heroine will return to her life as before, newly reminded of her true goal to rebuild the self-worth, which had been eroded through the willful cruelty of circumstance, on a foundation of strengthened self-knowledge. Our hero, however, may still not realize that he must find and accept himself in order to recognize his value; but as he searches for our hero, our hero is nowhere to be found.

ABOUT THE AUTHOR

Colette began writing poems, short stories, and novellas in grade school. Her interest in literature led her to marry her college English professor, but eventually a love of history encouraged her to trade up to a British historian. Technical writing dominated her career for twenty years, but finding little room for creativity in that genre, she is now a full-time author of fiction.

Pulse and Prejudice was named "A Most Inventive Adaptation" by Elle Magazine (April, 2016). It was the 1st Place Winner in its category in the 2013 Chatelaine Awards Romantic Fiction Contest and is listed in Chanticleer's *2013 Best Book Listing*. Colette dedicated 15 months traveling to Europe and Britain, researching Regency England and vampire lore and literature, to complete for historical accuracy. It remains faithful to nineteenth century literary conventions and Jane Austen's narrative to create a compelling, thrilling paranormal adaptation.

Colette was selected a "2013 Amazon Breakthrough Novel Award" Semi-finalist and named "Debut Author of the Year" by Austenprose for *All My Tomorrows*—now expanded and republished as *The Proud and the Prejudiced*—which was also chosen Austenesque Reviews "Favorite Modern Adaptation" 2013.

Colette's romantic thriller *Alicia's Possession* was the publisher's #1 Bestselling Romantic Suspense for 4 straight weeks following its debut in June of 2013 and then again in January, 2014, after being voted a "Top Ten Romance Novel of 2013" (P&E Reader's Poll). Colette is also the author of the controversial and erotic noir romantic suspense *Cartel Widow*, an Amazon bestselling new release.

Colette's latest novel is the sequel to *Pulse and Prejudice* entitled *Dearest Bloodiest Elizabeth*, which follows the newlywed Vampire Darcy and his bride Elizabeth from Britain to Antebellum New Orleans. Due to her devotion to historical accuracy, she devoted more than two years researching Creole Society and *Nouvelle Orleans* in the years following the War of 1812.

A bestselling and award-winning author under multiple pseudonyms, she is currently working on multiple projects including a parody of *Wuthering Heights* and a children's book based on the inspiration for the dog Amadeus from *Pulse and Prejudice* and *Dearest Bloodiest Elizabeth*. She lives in a lakeside community in South Louisiana with her historian husband and their two dogs.

www.ingramcontent.com/pod-product-compliance
Lightning Source LLC
Chambersburg PA
CBHW060151130626
46556CB00006B/2597